THE NIGHT HEROES:

RUNAWAY

THE NIGHT HEROES: RUNAWAY

Dr. Bo Wagner

Word of His Mouth Publishers
Mooresboro, NC

All Scripture quotations are taken from the **King James Version** of the Bible.

ISBN: 978-1-941039-04-5
Printed in the United States of America
©2018 Dr. Bo Wagner (Robert Arthur Wagner)

Word of His Mouth Publishers
Mooresboro, NC
www.wordofhismouth.com

All rights reserved. No part of this publication may be reproduced in any form without the prior written permission of the publisher except for quotations in printed reviews.

Runaway

"You sho you three young uns know what you gittin yoselves into? Master Feeney, he's a sho-nuf devil when he git crossed. Got a bad temper... as like to kill a man as speak to him. And don't think he gonna show you no mercy cause you kids; he'll cut yo throat as fast as he would three full grown men."

I just smiled at this dear old man, then calmly replied, "Joe, don't you worry about us. You just be ready to go come midnight. You are going to see your sweet Mabel again, and with God's power on our side, I pity Mr. Feeney or anyone else who tries to stand in our way."

Chapter One

Columbia, South Carolina, which was just outside our passenger side vehicle windows at the moment as we roared down I-26, is actually the state capital. I knew that as a geographical matter. But for the time being that was of little interest to me. My main interest was the tiny little mosquito flying around the middle seats of our Yukon, an annoying little pest that clearly had designs on my blood for his next meal.

"You got this, Kyle, you got this," a voice whispered beside me.

'Shhh, Aly, don't spook him," I said to my blonde haired, pint-size, lightning-in-a-bottle little sister, who had at least twenty-five-years' worth of impatience packed into her twelve short years of life thus far.

In the third row behind us, I heard another voice.

"Why do I suspect that this isn't going to end well…"

That voice belonged to my fourteen-year-old, raven-haired, certified genius sister, Carrie.

"Get thee behind me, Sister, thou savourest not the things that be of Kyle," I said with confidence as I focused ever harder on my target.

"Well, now, that certainly is an interesting twist on, or should I say twist *of,* Scripture."

That would be Dad. Through the years I have found that my dad is quite capable of multitasking, especially if that multitasking involves driving furiously like Jehu while simultaneously coming off with sarcastic quips.

The buildings continued to whip by as the sweat beaded up on my forehead. Like my dad, I am ultra-competitive and hate to lose at anything. It would be especially galling to lose when the contest at the moment was against a creature about one one-millionth of my size.

"Closer, closer, come on you little beast; you know you want it..."

And then, like a gift from God, he landed right on my forearm. Instantly I exploded into action, bringing my open hand down on my arm.

WHAP!!!

"Did you get him? Did you get him?!?"

I could see two things at once. The first thing I could see was my red and rapidly swelling arm. The second thing I could see was a mosquito buzzing towards the front seat, and I am pretty sure I heard him laughing at me as he flew that direction.

"No, Aly, I did not," I said with a disgusted grimace.

Snap! Went my dad's hand.

I could not believe what I just saw. But when he opened his hand and turned his palm to me, there was my horrible little enemy squished in my dad's palm.

Midair. My dad snatched him from behind his head out of midair.

Then he laughed. Sometimes I really don't like my dad even though I love him...

I looked down at my arm again and had to admit that, self-induced red mark notwithstanding, it was an above average arm for a sixteen-year-old. Certainly not as big as my dad's arms, he has been lifting weights for years, but still nothing to sneeze at.

I am Kyle, by the way, Kyle Warner. Along with my sisters Carrie and Aly, we are the Night Heroes.

My dad is a preacher. An evangelist, to be specific. He and mom have both been born-again Christians since way before any of us kids were ever born. When Dad was very young, God called him to preach. Once he met my mom, they went into evangelism. This means that my dad travels from state to state and city to city preaching the gospel to one church full of people after another.

And, since they also have kids to raise, we get to go along with them. That would make for an exciting life for any kids, even very ordinary kids. Imagine getting to see the Grand Canyon and the Statue of Liberty and the lovely mountains of North Georgia and a hundred other amazing sights!

But we three Warner kids are not ordinary kids, not by a long shot. Not only have we gotten to see all of the normal things that other evangelist's kids would get to see, but we have also gotten to see the battle of Chickamauga and Nazi Germany of World War II and the Moth Man himself. I know, I know, that doesn't seem to make any sense.

It's like this. A few years ago while on a meeting in West Virginia, we kids were awakened in the middle of the night by a voice calling our names. When we woke up, we were no longer in our own time! We had been transported back in time a century or more and were greeted by a train conductor telling us to hurry up and get on the train.

We learned a lot during that first mission. God calls us back in time to do work for Him, work that He over and over equips us to do. On that first mission, we rescued a little boy who was trapped in the mine by some bad men who were more than willing to harm him.

We have gone on to rescue a little girl from the Ravensbruck concentration camp, we have kept two brothers from killing each other during the Civil War, we have fought in the Indian wars of Tennessee in the late 1700s, we have dealt with a pirate off the coast of North Carolina, we have gotten wrapped up in a Mayan mystery that extended into North Georgia, and we have had the spiritual battle of our lives while facing the Moth Man in Point Pleasant, West Virginia.

Through all of these adventures, we have learned more and more about what we can do. We go to sleep each night and then wake up somewhere and sometime in the distant past. We have exactly five days to get each mission done. At the end of each day there in the past, we go to sleep and wake up back in our own time as rested as if we had had an entire night of good sleep. But if we get captured sometime in the past, we will not get to come home that night. That could be very hard to explain...

Also, if we get any injuries in the past, we would bring those with us into the present. We are, though, allowed to bring what we can carry with us back into the past. That has allowed us to carry some very helpful tools to get the job done.

Oh, and our second mission we learned that we are most definitely not allowed to bring anybody from the past into the present. That is strictly a no-no. We learned that one the hard way.

At six feet tall, I am bigger than the average sixteen-year-old, and way, way stronger. Dad has made sure our entire lives that all of us kids work hard and work out hard. He has taught us to fight. He has also taught us to think, and none of us picked that up any more thoroughly than Carrie. Like I said, she is our resident genius, and that big brain of hers has gotten us out of more than one very tight spot.

Columbia was now fading into the rearview mirror as we continued to make our way down I-26 East and then I-95 South. Our destination for this particular revival meeting was the Welch Creek Baptist Church located in Walterboro, South Carolina. This area of the state is what is called the Lowcountry. And I knew that once we got there, we would most definitely encounter some of the family, friends, relatives, in-laws, and outlaws of the little mosquito that my dad had so unceremoniously dispatched.

What I did not know is whether or not we would have any nighttime adventure. Sometimes we go for many weeks without hearing the call of the Conductor in the night. But we are ready, we are always ready. We are the Night Heroes.

Chapter Two

An hour or so past Columbia the Yukon began to slow, and Dad clicked on the turn signal for Exit 62. We got to the top of the exit and made a left on McLeod Road. A couple of minutes later it was a right onto Jeffries highway, then a right onto Keegan Drive, then a left onto Sidney road, then a right onto Welch Creek. Half a mile later we saw the church and the guesthouse and the large tabernacle in the side yard.

"One of my all-time favorite places," I heard my dad say happily.

I understood what he meant. We normally come here multiple times in the year, and it is always absolutely awesome.

Welch Creek is pastored by James Baker. He is in his late sixties, but the only way you would ever know that is by his snow-white hair. He is as wiry and energetic and lively as a teenager hyped up on Red Bull. He is also, as my mom always points out, one of the most gracious gentlemen you will ever meet.

Every April the church holds a large camp meeting there in the tabernacle. From Monday to Wednesday it will be jam slam packed with five or six hundred people. There will be singing and preaching and laughter and fellowship and amazing food, just an all-around great time.

Most years in the fall, Dad preaches a revival for the church as well. That is what would be going on this week, as Dad would start on Monday night and go through Friday night, and we would head out Saturday for our next destination.

As we pulled down the driveway for the guesthouse, I could feel myself unwinding. We actually stay there from time to time for a few days just as a getaway. It is very clean and comfortable, and the church, in its hospitality, allows a lot of different preachers to stay there during the year.

The Yukon slowed to a stop under the porch, and instantly everything erupted into a human beehive of activity. Suitcases were carried in, as well as the clothes that had been hanging on the bar in the back of the vehicle. Everyone knew exactly what room to go to and exactly what steps to take over the next hour. In under sixty-minutes time, we would all be unpacked, showered, dressed up in our Sunday finest, and walking across the parking lot to the Welch Creek Baptist Church.

It always amazed me to see that process, even though I had been part of it a thousand times. It was my mom, the heartbeat of the family, who was the engine behind all of this sixty-minute transformation. She could take a disheveled family of hobo-look-alikes and turn them into respectable churchgoers in an unbelievably efficient manner.

Naturally, Dad and I were always the first ones done and ready. Something about all of the primping and poofing and powdering and teasing and twirling and spraying and curling tended to make the girls a little bit later to be done than us guys.

But if I had heard him say it once, I had heard him say it a thousand times:

"Son, don't ever begrudge the girls their preparation time. One day when you get married, you will be glad girls take such pains to make themselves lovely."

Soon enough, though, we were all done and walking out the door. Forty-five seconds later we were walking into the back door of the church and were instantly greeted by friendly and familiar faces whom we had not seen in several months but regarded as family nonetheless.

My mom and Mrs. Baker and an amazingly sweet lady named Mrs. Jo Ann were quickly engrossed in a conversation along with several other sweet ladies. We kids were high-fiving and hugging and handshaking all of our buddies. Dad, though, was sitting on the front pew having a conversation, and it was clear that all his attention was intently focused on it.

I smiled because the person to whom he was devoting such attention was not the pastor or a deacon or a trustee, but the pastor's grandson, a boy named Noah. Dad will tell you quickly that he and Noah are friends, and he means it.

"Suffer the little children to come unto me," he will always remind us of what Jesus said.

I know that my dad can remember back to his own childhood, and he has told us of adults that sometimes made themselves friends to him, and he has told us the difference that it made in his own life. He has not forgotten that and is intent on doing for others what was done for him so long ago.

All of us spent a happy twenty-five minutes or so fellowshipping and catching up with all of our friends and meeting new people who had been saved and joined the church since the last time we were there.

At seven o'clock the service started. Welch Creek is not a big church, but they worship big. All of the singing somehow seems to come from heaven itself. People freely praise the Lord and testify of His goodness. Prayer requests are shared and prayed over, and it is evident that people genuinely care and are genuinely pouring their hearts out in prayer over the needs of others.

If you are ever anywhere near the area, this is a church that you do not want to miss.

At about 7:35 pastor Baker got up and introduced my dad, even though most everyone there knew him.

Two or three minutes later my dad was saying words that I have heard him say so very many times throughout my sixteen years, "Please open your Bibles…"

The passage that my dad read that night was from Mark 6, and the message he preached was *When a Saved Heart Isn't a Soft Heart*. The disciples had seen so many miracles, and yet over and over the Bible says that their hearts were hardened. It is sort of scary to think that even saved people are capable of having hardened hearts. I don't ever want to be that way; people need Jesus, and if they see Christians with hard hearts, they are far less likely to ever get saved.

Dad preached for about thirty-five minutes, which is about normal for him. He is not what a person would call "a long-winded preacher." But that thirty-five minutes was enough to get through to a whole bunch of people, and the altars were packed with God's children kneeling before the throne one more time, this time asking God to make sure that they always have tender hearts.

After church, we rode into town and grabbed a quick bite at Bojangles, then headed back to the guesthouse. As always, we prayed together as a family before going to bed. Those are precious, precious moments; no one should ever take them for granted. Then it was kisses and hugs all around, and then Mom and Dad went to their room, the girls went to their room, and I went to mine.

The bed was soft, the sheets were soft, the pillow was soft, and I thanked God that my heart was soft as well as I drifted off to sleep.

Chapter Three

The sound was slow and mournful. No harmony, just rhythmic voices singing from the depths of their souls.

O who will come and go with me? I am bound for the land of Canaan.

I'm bound fair Canaan's land to see, I'm bound for the land of Canaan.

O Canaan, sweet Canaan, I'm bound for the land of Canaan,

Sweet Canaan, 'tis my happy home; I am bound for the land of Canaan.

I'll join with those who're gone before, I am bound for the land of Canaan.

Where sin and sorrow are no more, I am bound for the land of Canaan...

Well, it sounded like there would be a mission this week for sure.

I slowly opened my eyes and found myself looking straight up into a lovely blue sky. Strange plants were waving gently in the breeze all around me. And then I heard the Conductor whispering my name.

"Kyle! Kyle! This way, over here."

I looked to my right, and through the plants, I could make out three fuzzy figures, one large one and two smaller ones. I knew the large figure would belong to the Conductor, and that Carrie and Aly would be the other two.

Not wanting anyone to be aware of my presence, I slowly rolled over to that side and made my way onto my knees. Then, as stealthily as an Indian I began to slowly crawl through the plants toward the tree line.

It took me about five minutes, and the singing continued as I moved, but finally, I slipped up beside Carrie, Aly, and the Conductor.

"Glad you decided to join us, Big Brother," Aly whispered sarcastically.

Carrie started to speak and add her two cents worth, but I interrupted her.

"Yes, Sis, I know I am always the last one to wake up. Some of us just have more stressful lives than others, I suppose, and therefore, sleep a little harder."

Her face instantly flashed with an "Oh no you DIDN'T just go there" look.

At that moment, the sources of the voices began to come into view. As I suspected from the sound, there were maybe a dozen African Americans, and all of them were in tattered clothing.

O who will come and go with me? I am bound for the land of Canaan.

I'm bound fair Canaan's land to see, I'm bound for the land of Canaan.

The workers were hoeing around the plants, carefully removing each and every weed anywhere nearby. The sun was somewhat low in the sky, but I could not tell if it had been up for an hour or so, or if it would be down in an hour or so. The wind continued to blow softly through the foliage, the workers continued to hoe and to sing their mournful tune. I could not exactly tell why, but it seemed at once to be a living picture both of sadness and of a strange sense of peace.

The peace, though, little that it was, was quickly shattered altogether.

"Canaan's land, is it? Bahahahaha! What makes you think God would even let you in? Canaan is a place for important people, not for low-down slaves."

My blood was boiling in an instant. I leaned to the left just a little to see who the arrogant voice belonged to and saw a man about my size on a horse wearing fine clothes and a wide-brimmed hat and holding a whip in his right hand. Underneath the brim of the hat, I saw two beady, evil-looking eyes, and I instantly had a desire to turn both of them black and swell them shut with a couple of well-placed jabs.

"Aw, Master Feeney, near as I can tell from the Good Book, God don't seem to care 'bout the color of no man's skin; He seems to love all equally and be willin' to take anybody in as one of His own."

That voice of reason came from one of the slave men who seemed to be about 50 years of age. And though he was careworn beyond his natural years, his face had a glow about it, a glow that I recognized very well. When people truly know Christ, they have peace that shines through the very worst of circumstances. I did not have a doubt in my mind that this dear gentleman was one of my brothers in Christ.

My thoughts were instantly snapped back to more temporal matters, though, by the harsh cracking of a whip, followed by the sound of a man wincing in pain yet trying not to scream. Whoever this Feeney character was, he had obviously taken offense to the true and biblical admonition of this slave beneath him. As quick as a cat his whip had cut through the air and laid a nasty, open, bleeding gash across the back of my newfound brother.

"And what would you know about the Good Book, Joe?" the man hissed. "Slaves cannot read and will never be allowed to read. All you know is what you have been told, and apparently, you have misunderstood each and every bit of that."

Normally, the next thing you would be reading here is that I was instantly out into the open dragging that jerk off of his horse and doing my best to pound his face into the ground. But the Conductor, apparently knowing that, had wrapped himself around me and was holding on tight. He had never done that before; he had never physically restrained me in any way. That being the case, I was absolutely stunned by how powerful he was. I literally could not move.

He leaned over and whispered in my ear, "Not yet, Kyle, not yet. You will get your chance, I assure you. But for right now, if you go out there, you will do far more harm than good. Bigger things are at stake than just a man getting a lash across the back. Trust me on this one, that dear gentleman has bigger needs, needs that only you and your two sisters can help to meet. Bide your time until you find out exactly what is going on and what you need to do."

I breathed out deeply, and my muscles relaxed, though my desire to cave the man's face in was still as hot as ever. But the Conductor had never led us wrong, and I knew that being our guide sent from God, he would not start now.

He let me go and began easing backward into the woods. We Night Heroes followed him, and as we did, I looked over and checked the faces of my two sisters. Their reactions were utterly predictable. Carrie had her forehead crinkled up, already thinking hard.

Aly, not so much. Her fists were balled up, her face was red, tears were streaming down her cheeks, and I knew that she wanted to destroy that evil man just as badly, maybe more so, than I did.

We walked on in silence for about twenty minutes. The ground seemed as level as if it had been paved. The foliage was thick, and everything seemed very humid and moist. Finally, we came to a clearing and saw two horses and a stagecoach that we assumed were waiting for us.

"You never do run out of new and interesting forms of transportation, do you sir?"

The Conductor smiled, and said, "Not yet, Carrie, not yet. But, if we go on many more missions, who knows, we may have to start repeating some.

"And now, before we go to our next destination, why don't we start like we always do. Carrie?"

"Yes sir, I know. Time and place. As to the time, I would say sometime just prior to 1861. Those slaves have not been emancipated, and it seems from the cocky attitude of that jerk slave owner that the Civil War has not yet even started. But based on the song they were singing, I would say we are not too far from the Civil War starting."

"Um, how in the world do you get that out of the song they were singing?" Aly asked with a confused look on her face.

"Because, Littlest Sibling, Canaan Land in the old African-American spirituals was actually coded speech; they weren't singing about heaven, they were singing about the freedom to be found up North in Ohio and other places. It was their way of encouraging one another that they may yet find a way to escape and get out of their bondage. If this was far back as say, the 1700s, they likely would not yet be singing those particular songs out in the field."

I looked over the Conductor, and he had that barely perceptible smile on his face that showed that he was once again impressed by my sister's powers of observation and reasoning.

"Continue, please," he said.

"Okay. As to the where, we have already established that we are in the South. But I think we can nail it down much better than that. As is normally the case, I would say we are not too far from our daytime domain, which in this case is Walterboro. We are very clearly still in the Lowcountry. The ground is flat, the soil is a mixture of dark dirt and sand, and the crops those slaves were working on is rice. That was the king crop in South Carolina pre-Civil War."

The Conductor smiled, this time fully, and said, "Well done, as usual, Young Lady. You are, in fact, just a few miles from

Walterboro. And the year is 1858. Those slaves you saw are currently the property of an unpleasant bully named Cornelius Feeney, whom Kyle has already expressed a desire to do some serious fist to mouth dental work on."

I smiled at that description. The Conductor had read my mind as clearly as if it had been written in boxcar-sized letters on the side of a mountain.

"And now," he said, "why don't you three kids climb aboard while I drive us to your next destination on this particular mission. I would recommend that all three of you get some rest along our journey; it is going to take us a while."

Carrie and Aly and I opened the door of the stagecoach, stepped up the two low-lying steps and crawled into the carriage. I sat on the seat facing forward and left the seat facing backward to the girls. No way was I going to be riding somewhere without being able to look ahead and see what was coming.

With a "Giddyap!" and the snap of the reins, the two draft horses effortlessly begin to pull the carriage forward. Within a matter of seconds, there was a quick and steady clip-clop-clip-clop of hooves on hard packed ground as trees begin to pass by us on both sides of the carriage.

The air had a sweet and lovely smell to it that any child of the South would immediately recognize as honeysuckle. I pity my northern friends, I really do, who have never had the experience to smell that smell or to pull that little center stem and taste that tiny sweet drop of heaven-made honey on each one.

We rode on in silence, and between the rhythmatic sound of the horses' hooves and the rocking of the carriage, combined with the sun rising in the sky, it did not take all three of us long to fall asleep.

Chapter Four

Since the tolling of the church bell and the sound of the horses' hooves hitting cobblestone happened at about the same time, I am not sure which of those things woke us up, maybe a little bit of both.

Carrie snapped awake a second or two after I did. Aly, who during an afternoon nap can easily sleep through a hurricane, continued to lay on Carrie's shoulder with her mouth hanging open.

"Hey, Aly, who is it that can't seem to wake up now?" I asked with a bit of smug satisfaction.

Her eyes popped open, and she began to look from side to side, clearly, just a bit bewildered.

"Is it morning yet? Have Mom and Dad gone down to the continental breakfast?"

"Um, Sweetie," Carrie said, "number one, we are staying in the house behind Welch

Creek this week, not a hotel, so there is no continental breakfast. Number two, we are currently in the year 1858, so there is no continental breakfast. Number three, it is well into the afternoon, so there is no continental breakfast."

"Sweet," Aly said with a grin, "let's look for some lunch!"

Metabolism of a hummingbird, that one.

The carriage pulled to a stop along the side of the street, and a second later the Conductor was coming around and opening our door. I stepped out, extended my hand to Carrie, helped her down, and then did the same thing for Aly. A rude young man will become a rude adult man, and a boy who will not be a gentleman to his sisters and his mother will probably also not be a gentleman to a future wife.

Once we were all out on the street, the Conductor waved his left hand toward the city that lay in front of us and said, "Well, here you are, Charleston, South Carolina."

Based on the position of the sun in the sky as opposed to where it had been when we first arrived, I estimated that we had slept for about seven hours, which would be about right by stagecoach with good fast horses from Walterboro to Charleston. In other words, no lunch for Aly.

"Thank you for the ride, Sir," Carrie said pleasantly. "Now, what are we to do from here?"

"I would recommend two things," he said matter-of-factly. "One, let the Lord guide you. Two, especially you, Kyle, avoid playing checkers when the devil is playing chess."

I had no trouble at all understanding the first one. And I sort of felt like maybe I understood the second one as well. I had a habit of thinking very simply; like when I wanted to dash out into the open earlier in the morning and rearrange that Feeney guy's face. But sometimes, actually often I suspected, the devil is thinking in much more subtle and detailed ways. My punching someone in the face would be like jumping a man in checkers. But if that is our strategy while the devil is utilizing bishops and pawns and knights and queens in elaborate patterns, we would get steamrolled and be of little help to anyone.

Without a word, we Night Heroes put our hands on each other's shoulders in a small circle and began this mission as we do each and every mission.

"Dear Lord," I prayed from the heart, "we know where we are, and we know when we are. But we do not yet know why we are here. And yet, we do know the God who has called us here. You have never failed to guide us and to help us as we strive to serve you. We pray for that guidance and that help one more time.

Please protect our parents back in Walterboro so many years removed from us. Please direct our footsteps and our eyes in this place and in this time. Show us the way to go, and let us see what you need us to see.

"Whomever we are here to help, Lord, please let us be completely successful in attempting to do so. We will glorify you, Lord, for any success that we have, knowing that it is You Yourself who has given us every ounce of strength and wisdom that we possess. These things we pray in the lovely name of Jesus, amen."

We opened our eyes, oh, so slowly, hesitant to leave the throne room of God. For a Christian, prayer is a way of placing ourselves in a very special way right into the presence of our Creator and knowing that kind of makes a person not want to leave.

When our eyes were opened, we looked around and, not surprisingly, the Conductor and the carriage and the horses were gone.

"Welp," Aly said in her inimitable way, "he's gone again, and we have a town to explore, so why don't we start starting?"

And then, without waiting for a response, she started walking down the street.

"I think she inherited that 'no fear gene' thing from Dad," Carrie said as she started after her.

"Probably," I murmured as I brought up the rear, "let's just hope she also inherited a little bit of mom's solid common sense."

Antebellum Charleston of 1858 was a lovely place. From history class I remembered that though its present location came about in 1680, Charleston was actually founded in the year 1670, making it the oldest city in South Carolina. Its original name was Charles Town, in honor of King Charles II of England.

I was amazed to realize that some of the structures and cobblestone streets I was presently looking at in 1858 had been there since shortly after the town was founded and would still be there even in what I considered to be the present day.

As we walked along the lovely streets, we passed by pine and palm trees, but especially the lovely angel oak trees that by our day would be the stars of Charleston. Even then they looked like something out of a J.R.R. Tolkien novel; branches sprawling all askew begging to be crawled on.

Unlike in our day, many of the buildings did not have signs on them advertising what they were. I guess it was just one of those situations where the locals knew what they were doing. We did see some bars, a few lovely churches, and an inn or two.

After wandering for about fifteen minutes, we turned onto Chalmers Street and came to a spot where there was both plenty of people and a good deal of noise. It was clear from all of the backs that we were staring at and the hands being raised and the fast-paced shouting and pointing that some type of business was being conducted. Up ahead we saw a lovely concrete constructed building with perfect archways and angles. Over everyone else's heads, I could just barely see the chest and head of a man facing the crowd speaking and pointing very quickly.

"It's Ryan's Mart," Carrie said, and the way she said it sounded like the weight of the entire world had just landed right on top of her heart.

"Ryan's Mart? What is that, Sis?" Aly asked uncertainly.

"It is a building owned by a former sheriff named Thomas Ryan. As of 1856, the city barred slaves from being bought and sold outside of the old Exchange Building because of traffic problems. Ryan secured this building for a slave mart, and it became one of the biggest ones. He made a fortune off other people's misery."

"So, you mean…" Aly said as her voice trailed off.

"I'm afraid so, Sis. All of this hubbub that we are watching is a slave auction. If we can get near enough to the front, we will be able to see it."

"No!" Aly said angrily, "I'm not going to watch human beings being sold like some toy off of a dime store shelf!"

"Easy, Pipsqueak, easy," I said as I placed my hands on her shoulders and bent down to look her eye to eye. "We are here for a reason, and I strongly suspect this is where we are going to find that reason. None of us like it, but if it was pleasant, there would be no reason for us to be here. God has a job for us to do; let's find out what it is and get it done."

She seemed to calm down at that, although with my volatile little sister "calm" is a very relative term.

Carefully, we began working our way through the crowd, nudging and then standing, then easing forward a little more, nudging just a bit more, and after twenty minutes or so we made our way to the front.

And as we did, it took about .0003 seconds for my blood to begin boiling over.

Inhuman. That is the only way that I could describe it. There were men, women, and even children chained to posts, waiting for their turn to be sold like some commodity. Their faces... some had a hopeless despair on them, some agonizing pain, some terrified fear. The only faces that bore anything that looked like happiness were the faces of those buying and selling; and even that happiness was not a pure thing, rather a dirty and sleazy thing, a "happiness" that could only be born of the wicked heart of man.

"Three seventy-five, I have three seventy-five, who will give me three eighty? Three eighty, three eighty, there! Three eighty on my right. Now, three eighty-five, three eighty-five for this fine young male slave, strong and healthy, three eighty-five, three eighty-five, yes! I have three eighty-five on the front. Now three ninety, now three ninety-five, three ninety-five, three ninety-five, back to the right! Now four, four hundred, four hundred, guaranteed money maker, four hundred, four hundred dollars for forty years of good service at least, who'll give me four, going once, going twice, sold, to bidder 121 for three hundred and ninety-five dollars."

Six. That would be the number of fists that were balled up in anger on three Night Heroes wanting to black two eyes of one smarmy little auctioneer.

"Checkers and chess," I whispered to both of my angry sisters.

We held our ground and watched as the next slave was brought forward. As difficult for us as the last one was, I knew immediately this one was going to be brutal.

It was a lady, probably in her mid-forties, with a sweet and lovely face etched with pain and sorrow.

"And now this asset, past childbearing age, but still with many good years of usage in the field left to her. We'll start the bidding at $100. One hundred there," he pointed, "now one-fifty, now one seventy-five, do I have two, two, who'll give me two, strong woman, good teeth, who'll give me two? Two! Right there, bidder number 349. Who'll give me two-fifty? There! I have two-fifty in the back, and now three, who'll give me three twenty-five, three twenty-five, three twenty-five going once... going twice... sold, to bidder 212."

Bidder 212, whoever he was, was apparently done with his shopping for the day. He walked onto the platform, took the chain that was wrapped around that dear woman, and began to walk away as if he was leading a dog.

"Come, woman," he said abruptly.

"Mabel," she said calmly and firmly.

"What did you say?" He asked as he whirled around to face her.

"I said, I have a name; Mabel."

The blow echoed off the concrete walls as he slapped her backhanded across the face. But she did not go down, she stood her ground, and calmly faced him eye to eye without saying a word, as blood trickled down her cheek.

"A few nights in the barracoon before we head to New Orleans should help to fix that uppity attitude of yours, woman," he said with a snarl.

Instantly Carrie and Aly and I looked at each other.

"You felt it too?" Carrie asked.

Aly and I nodded.

"She's the reason we are here," I said with certainty.

Now that we knew what was going on and had some idea of why we were here, we did not stay. None of us had the stomach or the desire to see any other human being so degraded. We slipped back out of the crowd and made our way down toward the waterfront. Across the way, we could see the almost completed Fort Sumter. I knew that in just three years the Civil War would start on this very spot. But right now, a war was waging in my heart, and I knew also in the hearts of my two sisters.

We found a spot under some of the ever-present low-lying brush, crawled far underneath it where we could not be seen, and went to sleep for our nightly trip home. This was going to be a physical and emotional battle; we would need all of the rest, all of the strength, and all of the information we could get our hands on in order to win it.

Chapter Five

The soft morning light of the Lowcountry was trickling through the curtain sheers into the window of my bedroom. I stretched and yawned and rolled over to hug my pillow for just a few more minutes. In the bedroom just past mine, I could hear Carrie and Aly begin to rustle about as they started their morning routine. Other rustling noises were coming from the kitchen, and I knew that would be Mom and her beloved coffee pot.

The "gnsnerkle" noise from the last room on the left was absolutely, certainly from Dad. Dad is far too unique to snore; he gsnerkles. That is the sound he makes when he is almost but not quite awake and laying on his back. I often wonder if mom would have married him if she had heard that noise before she said, "I do."

Within just a few more minutes the gsnerkling stopped, and I heard Dad's solid feet hit the floor. That "thud" let me know that I needed to be up as well. Even on the rare days when Dad is the last one up, he will be the first one ready to go, and woe unto the Warner who delays Mr. Impatience from his appointed rounds.

As I stared at my "bed head" in the mirror as I brushed my teeth, I thought of the scene of inhumanity from last night's mission and about the foolish notion that it was the way that God once expected it to be. Dad has taught us our Bibles well enough to know that anyone who claims the Old Testament had or even endorsed slavery like that of the old South is simply being dishonest. It was as different as night and day, so much so that people often decided that they loved their masters and never wanted to leave. Since the children of Israel had been genuine slaves in Egypt, God put a system of law in place that forbade them from ever treating anyone so unkindly. Everyone in Israel got the exact same amount of days off, the same holidays, and no one from the richest to the poorest was ever regarded as anything less than one hundred percent human.

I pulled my shirt on and brushed my hair, tightened my belt, tied my shoes, and was out of the room to meet the day. All five Warners converged in the kitchen, prayed to start our day, and then, were out the door and into the Yukon.

Ten minutes later we were pulling into the parking lot of the Olde House Restaurant. It is a fixture in Walterboro, and for a very good reason. Whether you are looking for lunch or breakfast or supper, the food will be delicious, and there will be plenty of it.

A few minutes later we five Warner's bowed our heads together one more time and were going to the Lord in prayer. We all joined hands and listened as my father prayed and thanked God for the food, and I was struck once again by how much it seemed like he was just having a normal conversation with his very best friend. That is exactly the type of relationship that I want to have with the Lord throughout my life as well.

When the prayer was done, we all made our way to the buffet and loaded up on eggs and grits and sausage and bacon, and some of us even hit the pancakes. I shudder to think how many tens of thousands of calories we consumed, but I also knew that we Night Heroes were more than active enough to burn them off. Don't worry about Mom and Dad; they are too. They may actually sleep at night unlike us, but during the day they very rarely slow down and always find the time to go somewhere and exercise.

We finished up breakfast, and mom paid the bill. Dad makes most of the money in the family, but he lets mom pay the bills and handle the day to day finances. She is very good at it, he always says, and he trusts her completely.

After that, we headed back to the guesthouse behind Welch Creek, and pretty quickly we had changed clothes and gotten ready for some good physical activity.

Our first stop was the gym and fitness center over near the hospital. Dad and I did chest exercises, and since that is his favorite thing, we were there for a little over two hours. Mom and the girls worked on the machines. Not too hard, though, since Dad had already let us know that we would be going for a run in one of his favorite places just after that.

We finished up our workouts, loaded up in the car, and just a few miles later were pulling up to the edge of a swamp, the Walterboro Wildlife Sanctuary.

We had been here many times before, and all of us loved it.

The Wildlife Sanctuary is six hundred acres of swamp with an amazing network of wooden boardwalks built all through it. For anyone who enjoys running, you will be hard-pressed to find a place quite as nice.

We exited the car, stretched once again for just a few moments, Dad set his running app, and we were off.

When it comes to weightlifting, I will not likely ever be quite as strong as my Dad, though I am very strong. But when it comes to running, I am already equal to him. Mom and the girls are both exceptional as well.

We started off at a good clip, and I enjoyed the feeling of the slightly bouncing boardwalks under my feet as we ran over water that was both black and lovely, stained with the tannic acid of the roots of ancient yet still standing trees.

The many birds in the swamp were not the least bit concerned with our presence. They were obviously very used to runners in their domain. Far off of the boardwalk, from time to time, I caught sight of deer carefully making their way from one patch of foliage to another.

All of us were breathing steadily and rhythmically and had settled into a pace that kept us pretty much together. From time to time there was a "swap!" as one of us swatted one of the many mosquitos that seemed intent on consuming us.

Halfway through our run, we crossed over the main road and into the second section of the refuge. Dad was pulling a bit ahead of us, so without a word we all kicked it up a notch and caught back up with him. I pulled alongside him, and we looked over at each other with that look...

And the race was on!

I stayed with him for the first thirty yards or so, then he, as he puts it, "caught another gear," and was soon out in front by ten or fifteen yards.

And then a minute later I zoomed past him as he slowed down and laughed uproariously. There was no way he could keep up that pace, and he knew it, he just did that to remind me that he "still has wheels."

And then I slowed to catch my breath, and mom and the girls came by both of us!

"Smart people run with the length of the race in mind," mom said with a bit too much glee as they left us behind.

Sure enough, thirty minutes later I arrived at the car to find them waiting for us, and Dad was right behind me. We all took time to catch our breath and then loaded up in the trusty Yukon and headed back for the guesthouse.

Showers; we all desperately needed showers. But since the guesthouse has two of those, and there are five of us, the two sweatiest got first dibs. That would be Dad and me. Somehow the girls came out of the workout and run almost glamorous. Smart females, those three.

An hour later we were all cleaned up and dressed and heading out for some lunch and further adventure. Lunch was Bojangles (Dad thinks there is never a bad time of day for a Cajun Fillet biscuit) and then it was into downtown Walterboro.

Our stop today, naturally, would be the Colleton Museum and Farmers Market. Dad,

Mr. History, would never miss a chance to learn about the history of an area.

As I thought on that, it dawned on me for the first time ever that perhaps that is one of the reasons we were chosen for these missions into the past anyway. Why would God bother sending people into the past if they didn't have a hunger to learn about it? That would make them fairly unuseful, I would think.

The museum itself is not large at all, but it still took us a couple of hours to go through. It has a lot of cool information about the rice plantation years and also a lot of displays about slavery. Carrie and Aly and I poured over those very carefully, soaking in every bit of information we could, knowing that may very well mean the difference between life and death for us or for others who needed our help.

There was one piece of information above all that we were looking for, all three of us. We had not even had to discuss it; every one of us was looking for something about a barracoon, the word that slave-purchaser had used last night.

Before you even wonder, no, we could not just "look it up on our phones." We three kids actually don't have smartphones, we don't need them since we are always with Mom and Dad, but they do let us use theirs if we ever need to. But even if we had asked, I doubted seriously that it would have helped. Remember, please, that we heard the word spoken, but did not see it *spelled.* Do you realize how many possible ways there could be to spell a word that sounds like that? Is it baracune, barracune, barakune, barrakune, bearacoon, bareacoon, baracoon, berucoon, berrecune...

You get the point.

And we did not find anything that matched that word. Nothing at all.

Mom did buy some really cool locally made jam, and Dad, surprise surprise, bought some locally made hot sauce.

We paid for our purchases and headed back out to the Yukon, and it roared to life as Dad turned the key. The next ten minutes were spent in a lighthearted jabbering back and forth, discussing all of the things we had seen, and then bouncing back and forth to discuss what we wanted to do tomorrow and for the next few days.

We got back to the guesthouse, Dad did a little bit of studying, the rest of us did some resting, and then before we knew it was time to meet Pastor Baker for supper. Somehow it did not surprise (or disappoint) me that we were heading back to the Olde House. Gone were the eggs and bacon and grits, and in their place was a salad bar, pork chops, fried chicken, green beans, macaroni, and much more.

And once again, all of it was delicious.

We ate and laughed and talked, but mostly we kids listened. When young people get a chance to be around someone like Pastor

Baker, and my Dad, of course, it is always good to do more listening than talking. They have so much wisdom... and a ton of corny jokes, too.

We finished up the meal, including dessert (did I mention the dessert? Banana pudding to die for...) and headed back to the guesthouse again. Five minutes later we were walking back across the parking lot and into the back door of the Welch Creek Baptist Church.

The floors creaked a bit as five sets of Warner's feet made their way into the midst of the auditorium. I really love old wooden church floors, covered in carpet or not. Something about them just seems to make me feel like Moses before the burning bush, finding out that he was walking on holy ground.

Folk started arriving in a fairly steady rhythm. And a lot of them were bringing bags and walking over to Mom and Dad to hand them to them. I smiled, knowing that those bags very likely contained awesome homegrown produce from these sweet folks' garden. And, in the case of Joe Ben, I knew there was a chance that one of those bags may well contain shrimp caught right out of the ditches in the old rice plantation he lived on and managed along with his wife, Jo Ann.

After a few happy minutes of backslapping and hugging and catching up on the day, the lovely strains of Victory in Jesus started emanating from the piano. That was our cue to head for our seats so the service could begin.

"Oh boy," began Pastor Baker with his signature phrase, "looks like this is going to be a good meeting. We certainly are planning on it, anyway. I'm here, you're here, but above all the Lord is here, and that really is all that matters."

And he meant it. Pastor Baker has been walking with Jesus for a very long time, and it is clear that they know each other very, very well.

After Victory in Jesus, it was At Calvary then a few announcements and then the offering. Each night of the meeting the church would pass the plates and people would give toward the love offering for my Dad. Dad never does and never will demand any kind of "up-front fee" for going to preach somewhere. I know for a fact that he would preach for free if needed, and sometimes he actually does.

Nonetheless, most churches we go in do their very best to take care of us, and Welch Creek is always exceptional at that. The church has caught the spirit of Pastor Baker's generosity through the years, and they have been a blessing to evangelists and missionaries alike.

After the offering and the fellowship there were a couple of great special songs, and then it was time for my Dad to come and preach again.

He took as his text Ruth 4:1-11. He explained the odd scene at the city gate where two different men had a chance to marry the same girl, and yet, they had very different reactions to her. Then he went back to the very beginning of the book and told the entire story of the book of Ruth from the time that Elimelech took his family into Moab all the way up to the beginning of chapter 4. He especially focused in on how Ruth made a choice, even though she could not possibly see how it could ever work out, to follow God and come to Bethlehem.

When she did, God opened up door after door for her and softened the heart of a man named Boaz toward her. Boaz was one of the men at the gate that day. The other man is just called, "Ho, such a one." That basically means, "hey, you there!"

That second guy was disgusted at the thought of marrying Ruth; Boaz was delighted at the thought of marrying Ruth.

The difference, as my Dad explained, was that the other girl in the book of Ruth, Orpah, made the opposite choice of what Ruth made. Since she could not possibly see how it could ever work out, she chose not to follow God to come to Bethlehem. If she had, God would have softened the other guy's heart toward her just like he softened Boaz's heart toward Ruth.

That really hit me right in the heart. I thought back to all of the times in my life when I was scared to step out on faith and follow God. And yet every time I did, God came through for me.

I looked over at my two sisters, the other two members of our team, and when their eyes met mine, I knew they were thinking very much the same thing.

We went to the altar that night, three evangelist's kids, three Night Heroes, and I knew that I was not the only one of the three asking God for forgiveness for the times I showed a lack of faith and thanking Him for all the times that He helped me to walk in faith even when it scared me to do so.

Soon the invitation was wrapping up, the closing prayer was said, and folks were milling about fellowshipping for a few more precious minutes before heading home. Carrie and Aly and I had slipped to a back corner of the church and were quietly discussing our coming task for the night.

"Do you think that Mabel is Joe's wife?" Aly asked.

"Oh, I suspect so, Squirt," I said with confidence. "But knowing that isn't going to help us any unless we can figure out what in the world a barracoon is."

"I never thought I would hear a word that I have never heard before," Carrie said. She was not bragging; she was just stating the truth.

That girl has read more books in her short lifetime than most people would read if they had ten lifetimes of eighty years apiece.

"What word is it?" A small voice from behind us said.

All of us jumped like we had been shot. We had been so engrossed in our conversation that we did not realize anyone had slipped up behind us.

When we landed, we wheeled around to see Noah, Pastor Baker's grandson. We all smiled like nothing was wrong, laughed a little bit, and then Carrie said, "Oh, just an odd word we heard recently, the word barracoon."

"Oh, you mean like the slave jails here in the old South?" he said.

Stunned, I knelt down a bit toward him and said, "What did you say?"

"Barracoon, that word you were talking about, I know it from my South Carolina history class. A barracoon was the slave jail that every slave market town had. Over in Charleston, it was on the same block as the slave market itself. They were bad places."

Carrie and Aly and I looked over at each other and smiled then looked down at Noah and said, "Thank you, Noah, we appreciate that. That helps us a lot."

And then he ran off to play with some of his friends. As he did, Carrie whispered to me, "That boy has no idea the huge thing he has just done. His paying attention in school history class is going to end up being the key to us saving that precious woman... and he will never know it till he gets to heaven."

A few minutes later five Warners were walking the lovely thirty-second walk under the Lowcountry stars back to the guesthouse.

Without having to be told, everyone started making preparations to bed down for the night. Teeth were brushed and flossed (Mom always says, "Only floss the teeth you want to keep." Great motivation, that.) night clothes were put on, and then we gathered for prayer one more time. Dad as most always led the prayer, while we four silently joined along. It is always cool to realize that no matter how many people are talking to Him at once, even those who are only talking to Him quietly in their head, God can hear and understand every bit of it.

And then there were hugs all around before we made our way to our rooms for the night. Mom and Dad, as always, would be getting some sleep. The girls and I made quick eye contact right before we disappeared into our different rooms; we knew would be seeing each other again within the next few minutes more than one hundred fifty years earlier.

Chapter Six

Rain. Why did it have to be raining? I don't like rain, especially when I am going to be spending a lot of time outdoors. And why did this rain have to be so odd? I like it when my nose stays dry, I really don't like it when it rains on my nose. But how was it raining on my nose and not on my head? And why had I not packed a nose umbrella like I normally do?

Wait a minute; there is no such thing as a nose umbrella. Come to think of it, there is no such thing as rain that only lands on a person's nose.

My left eye began to flutter open just a bit, and I willed my right eye to follow its example. When I did, I saw a blurry, skin colored cloud dropping one raindrop at a time...

On my nose.

Instantly I snapped awake with a gasp, and my two sisters erupted in peals of laughter. Aly waved her water bottle at me a couple of times and wiggled her wet finger in my direction. We were in the carriage, and from up front, I could hear the Conductor roaring with laughter as well.

"Sis, you are going to pay for this, I promise," I said with a devious smile, and I meant every word of it.

"No problem, Bro, do your worst, which will always be worse than my best, which I mean in the worst kind of way."

Ow. My still not-quite-awake head began to hurt trying to unravel that sentence.

"So, Night Heroes," the Conductor said as he leaned his head around the corner, "where would you like to start your day?"

We had not really discussed that, so we took a few quick minutes, huddled up, and discussed the issue.

Aly was all for going right back to Charleston and, in her words, "Kicking in faces and jail doors and walking away with that precious lady."

Carrie, the more levelheaded of the two girls by a wide margin, was absolutely against that.

"No, Sis, that's a bad idea. It would result in all of us ending up in jail, and Joe would not even know we had ever made an attempt. Checkers, chess. We have to come up with a plan that will allow us to do all of the following: spring her from jail before she is taken away to New Orleans, spring her husband from Mr. Feeney, reunite the two of them, and get them both to a place where they will be safe from now on."

"Agreed," I said quickly. "That being the case, I think we need to let Joe in on what we are planning and even enlist his help if possible. That means going to wherever he is, somehow managing to speak to him privately, and convincing him to trust us."

Both girls quickly nodded in agreement, and as we turned to speak to the Conductor, I saw that he was already smiling and nodding in agreement as well.

"That is a pretty good plan, I think," he said with satisfaction. "So, you are either going to need to go to the field or to wait till later and go to the plantation. What is your choice on that?"

"As much as I like doing things right away, I think the field in broad daylight is a bad idea. If I understand correctly from the books I have read, once the sun goes down the slaves were allowed to go to their own quarters and had the rest of the night relatively free. I would think that would be the best time for us to make our approach and the least likely time for Mr. Feeney to be watching."

"The plantation it is, then," he said with a smile. And then with a "giddyap!" and a pop of the reins the horses were off.

Today's trip was much shorter than yesterday's to Charleston. After an hour, the Conductor pulled the carriage to a stop.

We all got down out of the carriage and looked around to see nothing but trees. That did not worry us or surprise us a bit; it is exactly what we expected. We had done this enough to know that the last mile or two was going to need to be on foot so that no one would be aware that we were coming.

"Due east of here, two miles. The ground between here and there is level, but it has plenty of brush cover, so if you are careful you should be able to make your way to the edge of the property without being seen."

All three of us nodded and then without a word we knelt.

"Lord, one more time we come to You in prayer acknowledging our helpless dependence on You. Lord, we are strong, but not strong enough. We are fast, but not fast enough. We are smart, but not smart enough. In every way that matters, without You, we will never be enough. But Lord, with You we will never not be enough. Please give us everything we need to fulfill the mission to which You have called us. Give us wisdom beyond our years and courage sufficient to meet the task. These things we pray in Jesus' name, Amen."

The wind whistled slow and low through the brush and through the trees, landing on our cheeks as if it was a kiss from the throne room of heaven. We opened our eyes, and once again the Conductor was gone.

Without a word or sound, we hoisted our small packs onto our backs and started walking. We knew we could afford to go at an incredibly leisurely pace, unlike some of the other missions we have been involved in. We only had a mile or two to go and then it would be a watching and waiting game until the sun went down.

As we sauntered utterly silently through the brush, I knew that each of us was thinking our own individual thoughts, but toward the exact same conclusion. We three kids were all very different in many ways but all very much the same in all of the ways that mattered. There was a job to do, lives and futures were on the line, and every last one of us would give everything, including ourselves, to make sure that the job was done and done right.

That may sound overly confident, but it is really nothing more than the product of good training. My Mom and Dad have lived their lives in that exact same way in front of all of us. We have watched them sacrifice time and time again both for us and for friends in the ministry and even sometimes for total strangers.

I swatted a mosquito and immediately thought of my dad and his incredible mosquito grab in the vehicle on the way down to Walterboro. I smiled and shook my head, and whispered quietly to myself, "There is a lot more to Dad than meets the eye."

Aly, walking right behind me, picked up on that with what I call her "elf ears."

"That's true," she whispered, "but there is also a lot more to his kids than meets the eye."

"That is true as well," Carrie said from the back of the line, "but it is also true that there is a lot more to this pathway than meets the eye."

All of us stopped mid-step at that. Aly and I turned to face her, and I said, "What do you mean by that, Sis? What has your big brain picked up on?"

"Take ten normal-sized steps and tell me what you see," she said.

I know that sounds odd; it sounded odd to me, too. But if you have read any of our adventures so far, you know that very little escapes her attention, and that ninety-nine times out of one hundred she is not only right but has stumbled onto something incredibly important.

I turned straight ahead and counted out my steps. One, two, three, four, five, six, seven, eight, nine, ten.

"And?" I said in amused confusion, "there is nothing here. What is going on with you, Sis?"

"Are you sure there is nothing here?" she asked. "Look under your foot."

I looked down, and even though I knew we needed to be quiet, I could not help but laugh just a little bit. She was stretching this time, I mean really stretching.

"A flat rock, Genius? Seriously? We are out in the field, you do realize that, right?"

"I certainly do," she said with no hint of a smile on her face. "Now take another ten steps and tell me what you see."

I rolled my eyes but nonetheless started counting off steps again. "One, two, three, four, five, six, seven, eight, nine...

I could not believe it. It had to be a coincidence; my tenth step landed on another flat rock. I looked back at her, and the expression on her face had not changed. Without having to be told to do so, I took another ten steps.

Yep, another flat rock.

Aly was laughing and shaking her head. I was confused, very confused, but I knew there was something to this.

"Okay, Sis, what does it mean?"

"Well," she began, "I think we can figure that out by a simple process of elimination. It is obvious that the owner of the field would never put rocks in his field, flat or otherwise. It is also obvious that rocks at that regular of an interval did not just accidentally end up here. And they started way back inside the tree line where we began to walk. I am going to guess they lead all the way to the edge of Mr. Feeney's property. If they do, we will know that they have been placed there as markers, probably by some slaves who have either previously escaped or some who were planning to do so."

Genius. Not Carrie, she is a genius too, of course, but the plan itself. No one would even notice those stones unless they were specifically looking for them, no owner would ever think that there was anything devious going on if he happened to walk up on one. They were just rocks on the ground, and only someone like Carrie or someone who had been told of their meaning would ever notice them. If those stones led to a specified meeting place inside the tree line, it could well mean that we were dealing with a portion of the Underground Railroad, a network of people and places designed to help slaves escape to the North.

If that was the case, our mission might have just gotten simpler.

We started walking again, this time more quietly than even before. Sure enough, the rocks kept coming every ten paces.

After a while, the brush began to get more and more sparse. We got down on to our hands and knees and began to crawl the remaining hundred yards or so toward the edge of the property we had been approaching.

That last hundred yards took about half an hour; we could not risk any mistakes that close.

As we finally pulled up to the very edge of our cover, we lay very quietly and observed the surroundings. There was an incredible loveliness that I knew masked a hideous ugliness.

There was, it seemed to me, about a ten-acre clearing. To the west from which we had come there was the natural brush and undergrowth, and the tree line far beyond that. To the east and south, there were miles and miles of rice fields. To the north, there was a pathway leading off of the property and toward some ever so slightly rising hills in the distance.

In the center of it all, there was a lovely home; even by our modern standards, it would probably not be far from a mansion. It was three stories high with lovely white columns and porches and portico's at various places all around. Windows, there were windows on every side; <u>that</u> we needed to bear in mind.

Toward the very back of the property on the southern side, I counted six shanties; crumbling wooden homes that no doubt held far more people than they should have. This would be where the slaves lived.

On the far western side of the property, there was a large barn, and I knew this would house both the horses and the carriages that Mr.

Feeney and his family used, as well as whatever tools were used in the harvest.

The property was quiet; it was very quiet. I knew that there was likely a lady of the house somewhere inside making sure the female slaves tended to the domestic chores while Feeney and the men were gone. I would love to have gone exploring, but I knew we could not risk it; the very first thing we need to do was find a way to talk to Joe one-on-one.

And so, we did the thing that I hate the most; we waited.

If you are ever in a position where you have to lay on the ground in the Lowcountry during the daytime and not move for a very long period of time, let me tell you what you are going to feel like: a buffet bar for every bug within ten miles.

It did not take the three of us very long at all to be miserable. And yet we waited very, very quietly and very still. I snuck a look over at Aly, and, bugs and all, she had that angry, determined look on her face. I knew that she really, really wanted to tear Mr. Feeney down to size.

The hours passed slowly. I knew that Carrie was likely in her favorite place and doing fine, inside her own head. The fact that no one was talking was giving her plenty of time to think. Thinking for her is like candy for most other kids.

As for me, I alternated back and forth between praying and quoting verses in my head and wondering how my favorite team would do in the upcoming NBA season and thinking of how I would love to have a flamethrower to roast every bug in the entire field.

Finally, the sun began to go down behind us, and we heard the sound of rustling through the fields off to the south. And then we begin to see them shuffle onto the property and toward their little homes. Mr. Feeney and two younger men that looked a lot like him, probably his sons, I figured, came in behind them and shouted some instructions as they moved past them toward their glorious home.

"Be up early tomorrow, Cattle, we have plenty of work to do, and if I can't get any more out of you than I did today, I may have to put a few of you in my pocket."

As he said that, he laughed a wicked laugh, and his two boys joined him. Yep, they were his; they sounded like carbon copies of him. Now I had three people I wanted to punch in the mouth.

When everyone had gotten into their place and out of earshot, Aly looked over at Carrie and said, "What did he mean about putting them in his pocket? That doesn't make any sense."

Carrie dropped her head in sadness, and said, "He means to sell them off and put the money in his pocket. He is threatening to separate their families even further. It was always the most intimidating threat any slave ever faced. And they obviously know he means it, especially since we think he has already sold Joe's wife."

"So, what now, Kyle?"

"Now, Carrie, we wait just a bit longer. I want Feeney the Fetid to fall fast asleep."

"The Fetid?" Carrie giggled. "When did you become a big vocabulary person?" she asked.

"Hey, every now and then I like to learn new words, if only to try and understand you," I grinned back.

"Fetid? Like the cheese?" Aly asked in confusion.

Both Carrie and I had to put our hands over our mouths to mute our uncontrollable laughter; we could not afford to draw attention to ourselves. Finally, when we could breathe and speak without erupting again, Carrie said, "No, Aly, you are thinking of Feta. Feta is a cheese; fetid means stinky."

"Ohhhh," she said with amazement, "I like that! Fetid, fetid, fetid...."

I knew we would be hearing that word a lot for a while.

Chapter Seven

When the sun finally kissed the horizon, we Night Heroes began to stir, getting ready for our next move. I knew that within a half hour or so, it would be safe (relatively speaking) to try and make contact with Joe. How in the world to do it, though, that was the question. I remembered very well from reading through the book of Exodus that when people have been in slavery for a long time, they are often as quick to turn on their would-be deliverers as their captors. When Moses tried to free the children of Israel from Egypt, it did not take them long at all to side with the evil Pharaoh against him.

We really needed to find a way to speak to Joe individually, rather than trying to approach an entire household full of people.

"Why don't they just all run away at night?" Aly asked. "It doesn't seem like anyone is looking."

"A couple of reasons, Sis," Carrie said quietly. "One, where would they go? Most everyone for hundreds of miles around is on board with slavery, so they have no refuge nearby. Two, there are actually roaming bands of government-appointed rangers, for lack of a better word, who are always on the lookout for runaway slaves. If any one of them were to leave tonight, it would be known by early in the morning, and by tomorrow night they would be dragged back in chains and beaten to pieces. They may as well be in a maximum-security prison surrounded by high fences and razor wire."

"So how are we going to have any success in this?" Aly asked in frustration.

"Hard, fast, and long," I said.

"What?"

I turned to her and patiently replied, "We hit hard, we go fast, and we go long. We put a plan in place, and when we begin to execute it, we move farther and faster than the enemy could ever anticipate." Then I smiled and said, "And, we look for the Lord to give us openings… just like that one."

The girls turned their gaze to follow mine, and I heard both of them gasp as they saw what I saw. Halfway between one of the shanties and the brush we were hiding in was old Joe, with his knees on the ground and his face and hands stretched heavenward.

"Lord, You done promised to do good to Yo servant," he said in a low, sad, voice. "But Lord, my hearts a-breakin right now. I cain't go on without my Mabel, Lord, You done seen that. Lord, Master Feeney don't know You, but I do. I know what You capable of. If You so will it, You can help me git to her. Lord, please don't let em take her down there to N'orleans. If'n they do, I'll never see her agin. Lord, if'n that's Yo will, I'll do my best to praise You through my tears. But Father, if You would, please don't let it go that way. Even now I know You Lord in heaven and earth, and no man can stand ag'nst Yo will. So will it, Lord, will for me to git my Mabel back somehow. I pray all this in Jesus's name, amen, and amen."

Old Joe left the throne room and dropped his eyes back down toward the earth. And then he saw the dot.

It was a risk, that's for sure. How would a person from the 1800s react to a green laser dot mysteriously showing up on the ground in front of him? Would he scream and draw unwanted attention? Or would he...

He reached for it.

Aly moved it slowly in front of him another foot or so and stopped. The sweet old man stood and looked at it; he was clearly perplexed.

"Come on, Joe, come on," I said in my head, "follow it, understand..."

He took a step toward it, and Aly moved it another length away. He took another step, and she moved it again. And then, as if he somehow grasped that the dot wanted him to follow, the pace picked up. Step, move, step, move, step, move, step, move, until the dot, and Joe stopped just inside the brush line, just six feet away from us, but still unable to see us.

I had to take the next chance. I had to speak and hope Joe would not cry out. That being the case, I had to choose my words perfectly. Checkers, chess. Fortunately, I was pretty sure I knew just the thing:

"Call unto me," I whispered, "And I will..."

Joe finished the words with me "answer thee and show thee great and mighty things, which thou knowest not."

"So, what bush in the middle o' the night is wantin' to remind me o' the words of the prophet Jeremiah, and how is that bush makin' a green dot on the ground?" he said with a pleasant touch of humor in his voice.

We Night Heroes stood up and faced him.

"Hello, Joe," I said quietly. "We bring greetings from the King of kings."

We didn't have much time, I knew that, but I also knew we had some explaining to do, at least as much as we were allowed to do.

"You don't know us, Sir, but we are family. I heard you out in the field yesterday talking to Mr. Feeney about the Lord, and though I hate to listen in on a man's prayers, we also listened to you just now talking to your Father and our Father. Well, Joe, He is the reason we are here, and I suspect that your prayers are why He has sent us. My name is Kyle, Kyle Warner. These are my sisters, Carrie and Aly.

"Joe, we were in Charleston late yesterday."

I hated to say this next part, but it had to be said.

"We saw your Mabel being sold."

As I said those words, a cry of anguish escaped his soul. "Oh, Mabel, sweet Mabel, dear God, what shall I do?"

I quickly calmed and quieted him.

"Joe, she is why we are here; you are why we are here. We intend to get her out of the barracoon and you off of this plantation and the two of you to safety, together."

"The barracoon! How did she end up there, what happened?"

I told him about her calm and composed insistence that she had a name.

"Yep, that's my Mabel," he said with a chuckle, "never did have no fear of nothing or no one."

"Her doing that and ending up there is going to work to our advantage," Carrie said firmly. "It lets us know right where she is and where we have to release her from. So as long as you are here and she is there, for the time being, we have to hope."

Joe looked so very skeptical that I had to interject, "Don't look so worried, Friend. God sent us here for this purpose. Two nights from now, at midnight, you need to be ready to go. Take the escape path marked by rocks up into the tree line, and we will be waiting for you with Mabel."

He looked positively stunned when I mentioned that path and immediately began to back away from us.

"Who is you, really? Ain't nobody know about that path but us, and it ain't been used in years. You somebody that knows somethin' and trying to set us up, you tryin' to get me sold off too?"

If Carrie had not stepped in right at that moment, things would quickly have turned into a disaster.

"Nobody told us about the path, Joe, I figured it out myself just by observation, just like I figured out that you are left-handed and partially blind in one eye. Every time you gesture it is with your left hand, and you have consistently turned your head a little bit past center to look at whoever is talking to you out of one eye."

I had not noticed any of that. Looking at Aly's face, I knew she had not either. Looking at Joe's face, I knew that he hadn't told anybody any of those things, ever. The part about the eye, especially, would have made him far less valuable of an asset, and much more likely to be gotten rid of.

Joe smiled and shook his head in amazement. "Whoever you is, God done blessed you with an above average mind and a keen eye. I apologize, it's just a body doesn't much know how to trust these days."

"I understand that, Joe, I really do. But please believe me when I tell you that you can trust us. Remember what I said and be ready."

Joe smiled and shook his head one more time and said, "You sho you three young uns know what you gittin yoselves into? Master Feeney, he's a sho-nuf devil when he git crossed. Got a bad temper... as like to kill a man as speak to him. And don't think he gonna show you no mercy cause you kids; he'll cut yo throat as fast as he would three full-grown men."

I just smiled at this dear old man, then calmly replied, "Joe, don't you worry about us. You just be ready to go come midnight. You are going to see your sweet Mabel again, and with

God's power on our side, I pity Mr. Feeney or anyone else who tries to stand in our way."

A moment later the sweet old man was hobbling back toward his shanty, and my sisters and I were heading up into the tree line to catch our nightly trip home.

Chapter Eight

It was a wet day in Walterboro that we Night Heroes woke up to. It is funny how a rainy day always makes people move a little slower in the morning. Even Dad seemed to be yawning and shuffling a bit.

"Good grief, sleepy heads," Mom said in amazement. "All of you are acting like zombies this morning."

"Well, sweetie," Dad said groggily, "we zombies have not had the four cups of coffee caffeine boost that you are currently enjoying. Give us a few moments, and I promise we will be a bit more lifelike."

Half an hour worth of showers later, all of us felt a bit more human and went in search of breakfast.

"Where are we headed?" Mom asked as Dad pulled out of the driveway.

The next words were beautiful words, lovely words.

"Cracker Barrel, Sweetie. Pastor Baker is going to meet us there for breakfast."

Cracker Barrel. Just one more proof that there is a very good God in heaven. They can be found at decently sized exits all along interstates across the southern United States. Every meal will always be wonderful no matter which location you are in. And, while waiting, you can play giant checkers in front of the fireplace.

A few minutes later we pulled into the Cracker Barrel, disembarked from the trusty old Yukon, and went inside. Pastor Baker was waiting for us, and a few minutes later we had taken our seats. We ordered our food, then we three kids went and played some checkers while the adults talked around the table.

It almost felt a little bit weird playing checkers since we had spent the last couple of nights playing chess.

Soon enough the food had arrived, and a mountain of eggs and pancakes and French toast beckoned us back to the table. The next thirty minutes were a glorious time of food and fellowship, listening and laughing. And, since the rain had cleared out and the sun was gloriously shining again, there was a wonderful and pleasant surprise to come.

"Would you folks like to go to Edisto Beach and spend a couple of hours today?"

Oh, Pastor Baker, that will be an easy answer for my dad, Mr. Beach.

"Absolutely!" Dad said excitedly. "You had me at 'beach.' How far away is it?"

"About an hour or so," Pastor Baker said, "and it's a pleasant, off the beaten path kind of place."

Perfect, just perfect.

We finished up the meal, left a very generous tip (always leave a good tip; waiters and waitresses have a very hard job), paid for the meal, and headed out. It was mostly back roads on the way there, and Pastor Baker rode with us in the Yukon so that we could all talk and fellowship together.

The pine trees and palm trees of the Lowcountry whipped by. From time to time Pastor Baker would have us pull off down the side road and show us someplace of significant meaning from his early ministry. But soon enough we were pulling into the tiny town of Edisto Beach. It is a really unique little place; it is not at all commercialized like Myrtle Beach or something of that nature. Just a few little businesses here and there, a pizza shop, and then a lot of cottages right on the beachfront.

We parked in the public parking, kicked off our shoes, and went for what my dad calls "sun, sand and sea therapy." We soaked in the sun, buried our toes in the sand, picked up seashells, waded calf deep out into the surf, and just enjoyed the beauty of God's gem of creation. Seagulls drifted lazily in the breeze, and from time to time we could see the fins of porpoises breaking the water a couple of hundred yards offshore.

I am pretty sure all of us see eye to eye with Dad on this one; if we didn't have somewhere else to be, we could stay on the beach forever.

But forever is a very long time and would take us well past time for service tonight, and, incidentally, an important mission we had to attend to after dark.

So, it was that we all loaded up a few hours later and headed back toward Walterboro, grabbing a late fast food lunch along the way. We dropped Pastor Baker off back at the Cracker Barrel where we had left his truck and then headed back to the guesthouse to get cleaned up for service.

An hour later we were walking into the back door of the Welch Creek Baptist Church one more time. The crowd was growing each night, and we were excited about what the Lord was doing in this place.

When it came time for the preaching, Dad took his text from James 5:7-11. It is a New Testament passage, but it references an Old Testament character, the man called Job. Thousands of years after his death, Job was still such a significant man in people's thinking that James included him and referenced him in the book he wrote.

You can read Job's story in the book that bears his name. My dad's message was about the fact that after all Job went through, the Bible says that he lived, and he lived for a great many years longer. He had many times along the way where he said that he didn't want to live because he thought that things would never get better in his life. And yet, the God who has the ability to take us to heaven where everything is perfect also has the ability to make things better in this life. And for Job, he did. Never, ever give up on life, no matter how hard it may seem. If God can make things better for Job, He can make things better for you, too.

The message seemed to touch the hearts of a lot of people, and there was a lot of crying around the altar as people poured out their burdens to the Lord.

The service soon came to an end, and since one of the ladies had brought us a meal that she had cooked in her home earlier, we went back to the guesthouse and enjoyed that before bed. Catfish stew (if you have never tried it, trust me, you do not know what you are missing) cornbread, pinto beans, and peach cobbler. Basically, culinary heaven.

We cleaned off the table and then headed to the various restrooms to prepare for bed. Once all of the flossing and brushing and rinsing and pajamaing (I am pretty sure I should not be making a verb out of the word pajama, but I do so anyway) was done, we met together for prayer as a family one more time, and it was off to sleep for all of us, even though three of us obviously would not be asleep for long.

Chapter Nine

"I hope you don't mind," the voice of the Conductor said, "I took the liberty of starting us out toward Charleston since I assumed that is where you would want to go first today."

We Night Heroes opened our eyes and stretched and looked out of the carriage to see the trees moving past our doors.

"That's perfect, sir," I said. "Thank you so much for doing that."

"No problem," he responded pleasantly, "I figured you could use a few extra minutes of sleep. We are still a good ways out of Charleston, so you have time to talk together and formulate your plans for the night."

And so, we did. We knew that, though the task was hard, we had some advantages based on the time period. If this were our day, as soon as there was a jailbreak people would be on television and social media spreading the word far and wide. But since we were in the 1800s, even after we sprung Mabel out of jail, word of that may not reach the plantation for days. That would be an advantage that we would sorely need.

Once we reached the outskirts of Charleston, we stopped and made some further plans, and they required a favor from our Conductor.

"Sir, we have a need. We know that as soon as we are done praying, you are gone, and the rest of the task remains up to us. But would it be possible for us to borrow the horses and the carriage? That would certainly keep us from having to do anything unpleasant and unchristlike like, say, 'borrowing' someone else's horses and carriage without their permission."

"Oh, I think that will be just fine," he said, "but do any of you know how to drive this thing?"

"Welp," Aly said with a scrunched-up face, "they don't exactly have this arrangement in Drivers' Ed, so that would be a no…"

The Conductor laughed and then gave us a quick crash course (wow, that is a horrible way to put it; I hope it is not prophetic) on how to drive a horse and buggy, and then we knelt to pray.

"Lord, one more time we come before You, seeking Your face and asking for Your favor. Tonight, we are going to try to break a dear woman out of jail, a woman that has no business being there to begin with. We are fighting both steel and sin, culture and concrete. Please help us to do everything we do absolutely successfully on this night. Blind the eyes of the enemy to our presence, make them unaware that we are even here, shield our doings from their eyes. May our horses be swift and sure, and when this night is over let us be one step closer to accomplishing the task that You have sent us to do. These things we pray in Jesus's name, Amen."

When we lifted our eyes, the Conductor was gone, but the horses and carriage remained.

"My brother, my brother, the chariot of heaven, and the horsemen thereof," Carrie said with a grin.

"Nice, Sis; let's just hope your very paraphrased reference to 2 Kings 2 does not indicate that any of us will be going to heaven just quite yet. We still have work to do."

We secured our ride and made our way into town. Our first task was to locate the barracoon, which should be very easy now that we knew where to look. Breaking Mabel out of it? Now that would be another thing entirely, but I was already working on a plan.

The loveliness of the town seemed so out of place, so contrary to the ugliness of what was happening. We clopped along on beautiful cobblestone streets, and I thought of the ugliness of the feet of human beings shackled in chains. We passed by lovely trees, made by the hand of our good God, and I thought of the ugliness of people being hanged on those same trees.

"Kind of sad, isn't it?" Carrie asked. "It just doesn't fit."

I smiled. By now it did not surprise me in the least to realize that my ultra-perceptive sister had practically read my mind and was thinking the same thing I was thinking.

As we rounded the corner a block away from the Ryan's Mart, we stopped and took in the surroundings. People were milling about doing their daily business, carrying produce, chatting about politics, oblivious to the fact that three very disruptive kids were in their midst, and about to break a bunch of eggs on the way to making an omelet. Without a word we began to circle the building, sauntering nonchalantly, but soaking in every detail.

As we rounded the back corner of the block and started down the street, I knew we were in the right place.

O who will come and go with me? I am bound for the land of Canaan.

I'm bound fair Canaan's land to see, I'm bound for the land of Canaan.

O Canaan, sweet Canaan, I'm bound for the land of Canaan,

Sweet Canaan, 'tis my happy home; I am bound for the land of Canaan.

*I'll join with those who're gone before,
I am bound for the land of Canaan.*

Where sin and sorrow are no more, I am bound for the land of Canaan...

The words were sung low, sadly, and without hope. Row after row of barred windows emanated the sound.

"They know it's not going to happen; they are singing out of a strong will, not out of actual hope," Aly said with a mixture of anger and sadness.

"Oh, I don't know, Pipsqueak, some of them may just make it after all."

She looked up at me and grinned, mostly because I was grinning too, my "I'm going to enjoy every minute of the trouble I'm about to cause" grin.

"I know that look, Bro, and I like it. Is it finally time for the Vaseline, a box of sparklers, and a bottle of Tabasco sauce?"[*]

I just laughed. "No, Littlest Sis, whatever you had and have planned with all that, I still don't think this is the time. I have something a bit different in mind."

"Rats. It would be epic."

"I am sure it would, Squirt. I am sure it would."

Carrie had been quiet thus far, and that was not a surprise. I knew that she was doing

---

[*] See <u>Cry From The Coal Mine</u> to find out about that

the same thing she did in the TNT area when we dealt with the Moth Man; planning and mapping.

We finished our lap around the building and around the block, and then casually made our way down to a huge tree a quarter mile down the street and sat down like three kids just whiling the day away. To complete the picture, I pulled out my Buck knife and started whittling on a piece of wood.

"So, Carrie, watcha got? Let's compare notes and thoughts."

She started in immediately and efficiently. "One: getting a single person out without all of the others knowing about it and crying out for help and drawing attention to us will be impossible. Two: the fact that the barracoon is on the backside of the street is certainly an advantage, especially if we can cause some kind of distraction on the front side. Three: every person in there is "being punished," as if being enslaved is not punishment enough. They are all chained to the wall, stretched out and in pain. Four: the padlock on the front door, even though it is not exactly modern, is huge. Cutting it is out of the question, I think."

"I can add one to that," Aly said. "Even if we spring everyone, how will we manage to grab Mabel and convince her to come with us?"

"Good observations, Carrie, and good question, Aly. So let's take all of that in order.

As to getting a single person out, you are correct, that would be impossible. It would also, from my perspective, be undesirable. Think Steve McQueen and the Great Escape."

Carrie smiled. "I like it. You want to pull a World War II type of escape; spring everybody so that the authorities have to spread all their resources looking for dozens, not just one. Go on."

And I did. "As to your second point, yes, it is an advantage, and yes, we are going to need a distraction. Which is why I intend to blow up one of those ships out in the harbor."

Both Carrie and Aly did a double take on that one.

"Um, would you mind repeating that to make sure I heard you right, Kyle? For a second there I thought you said 'blow up a ship in the harbor.'"

"That, my brainiac Sister, is exactly what I said. Once it gets dark everyone in this wicked place will be up here in town, and most of them will be getting drunk and having a grand old time. Because of the political turmoil, and the risk of war, I guarantee you that those boats are loaded with gunpowder. I intend to fire the first shot of the Civil War a few years ahead of time. Mind you, everyone will think it is just an accident, but when that boat goes boom, there will not be a single soul in this town that doesn't head down to the water to see what is going on."

Carrie smiled just a bit, and said, "I like it so far. Please, continue."

"Okay. As to point three, tell me, Sis, did you happen to look at the relative size of the lock and/or chains people were held to the wall with?"

"Of course, I did. The keepers have put all their money into the lock on the front door, I would say. The locks holding the captives to the walls are actually not that big."

"Good," I said as I pulled a pair of bolt cutters from my pack, "then this should do the trick for them. How many were there?"

"Twenty-two."

"Twenty-two, or twenty-two-ish?" I asked.

Carrie just cocked her head to the side a bit and raised her eyebrows at me.

"Got it. You don't do 'ish.' Twenty-two exactly."

"As to number four, Aly, I think you have probably noticed your pack is a bit heavier than normal. How about pulling out the small car jack for me."

"So THAT'S why this thing feels like a pig tonight! You could have just asked me to carry it, you know. But why a car jack? It's not like anyone here has any flat tires to change."

"The jack is not for a tire, Squirt. When we were in town the other day, I happened to pay attention to the doors. Every last one of them are simply heavy doors slid down onto upright hinges. That main door that the keepers took such care to padlock, it probably weighs four hundred pounds or more. But this jack will lift it right off the hinges. As to your question, Aly, we will leave Mabel to Carrie; I would say she knows what to do."

With our plans in place, we put our tools back in our packs and waited. The sun was getting lower on the horizon, and soon it would be time to start the fun.

Chapter Ten

As the daylight got smaller and smaller, the crowd in the town got bigger and bigger, and noisier and noisier. The girls and I had talked details for the last little while, and, with a nod, we all got up and spread out to our assignments.

I made my way through town and then sauntered down toward the harbor. I knew that in just a few years this would be the very spot that the deadly Civil War would start. But that was not my issue; my issue was to start a mini-war tonight as a diversion.

Once I got down to the water I looked around carefully and, sure enough, the place was deserted. Large ships were far out in the harbor, and small docking boats were tied in rows by the shore. I went to a nondescript little boat, untied it, and settled in for a little row. Dipping paddles very quietly into the water, I rowed out to what was clearly a fighting vessel and would therefore surely have stores of gunpowder.

Since no one was aboard, there would be no one to lower the gangplank for me. No matter; I had climbed chains to get aboard ships before. In under two minutes, I had shimmied up the chain and was standing on deck. The salty breeze kissed my face, a greeting from heaven bidding me blessings in my work.

Quickly I made my way down the hatch and below deck. I clicked on my little LED flashlight and made my way down the dark passage, with ancient boards creaking under my feet. "Not nearly as nice as the floorboards at Welch Creek," I said to no one in particular.

But then, horror of horrors, a voice answered!

"Welch Creek? What's a Welch Creek, Mate?" The lantern came on about the same time as the voice spoke, and a man walked right around the corner and stood face to face with me! Apparently, someone had left a guard behind to watch the boat!

I had no choice; I had to react instantly, or all would be lost. I shined my light in his eyes and shot out a front kick right to where I knew it would immediately double him over. And it did. Then I dropped an elbow on the back of his head, and he was immediately out cold. I was just glad his lantern did not break when he fell; I did not need a fire just yet, I needed an explosion.

But now I clearly had an additional problem; I had to get this guy to safety on top of everything else.

I raced to the powder room and pulled my firework fuse line out of my pouch. I had planned on using five feet, which with my slow burn fuse would give me two and a half minutes, but now I scrapped that idea and went with fifteen feet instead, for seven and a half minutes. I put one end of the fuse in a barrel of powder, lit it, and raced back down the passage. I picked up the still very unconscious guard, threw him over my shoulder, and carried him up on deck. Boy, I was glad this was not a big man, or I would not have made it in time!

Once up on the deck, I tied a rope around the man's legs, lowered him over the side, and down into the boat. Then, knowing time was precious, I bypassed the chain and just jumped.

Man, that water was cold!!!

Biting my lips to keep quiet, I crawled over the edge and into the boat and started rowing like mad for the shore. I got the boat there, tied it up, then used a length of rope to tie up my unconscious enemy and to gag him as well. I hauled him a safe distance away, put him under some bushes where he would not be immediately seen, checked my watch, and raced for the barracoon. I had just rounded the corner when I heard the explosion:

It sounded like a nuclear bomb had gone off! I looked back behind me and could see a huge fireball rising up into the night sky. I heard glass shattering, and I knew that any windows facing the harbor were probably gone. People immediately poured out of every building and started running for the harbor.

We had to hurry. We REALLY had to hurry!

Carrie and Aly were already at work. They had the jack under the base of the door and were winding it up. I jumped in and grabbed the crank and took over. In about sixty seconds we had the door lifted off of its hinges, and, pulling it and the jack simply moved it to the side. Aly already had her flashlight out. All of the captives were murmuring and rustling, and Carrie urged them to quiet down while I went to work.

"Snap!" went the first lock, and a boy who looked to be about fourteen was free. Carrie helped him into a standing position. "Snap!" went the next lock, and an older woman was free, and Aly was there for her. Five more snaps liberated three young ladies, a young boy, and a man of about thirty rippling with muscles. Fifteen more snaps to go. I got through the next three – and realized that snapping locks, even for someone as strong as myself, was hard going! I was slowing down when I needed to be speeding up, and that made me start to feel the panic rising in my throat.

"Hand me the cutters, young man, you've done some mighty fine work, but you gittin' tired. Let me take over."

It was my new, muscle-bound friend. Snap. Snap. Snap. Snap. Snap. Snap. Snap. Snap. Snap. Snap. Snap. Snap.

Free. They were all free! But they were all also standing around not sure what to do.

Carrie was already talking to Mabel, whispering in her ear, and the sweet lady was nodding, and then reached out and hugged both her and Aly. I knew that had gone well, so I quickly spoke to everyone else.

"You don't know me, and you don't need to. All you need to know is that I have been sent here by the King of Kings, the Lord Jesus. I have caused enough of a distraction that you will have a sizable head start. What you do with it is up to you. I would recommend that you split up by twos and threes and make your way North. Keep to the trees and swamps, travel only by night, lay low during the day. Run as if your lives depend on it; for they do."

They did not have to be told twice. In thirty seconds flat, they were gone. We followed them out, then I turned to move the door back in place. Carrie immediately figured out what I was up to and joined in.

"What are you guys doing?!?" Aly hissed.

"Buying time!" Carrie hissed back. "If we put the door back, even when everyone comes back into town, they will think all is normal here. That will buy these folks hours and hours worth of a head start till anyone even realizes they are gone. Get Mabel to the carriage, we will be right behind you!"

Aly raced off with Mabel, though as stiff as that sweet lady was from being chained upright, "raced" was a relative term. Carrie and I got the door back in place, grabbed the jack, and caught up with them about the time they got to the carriage. The girls climbed in, I untied the horses and got into the driver's seat, and with a frantic "Hyaaa!" and snap of the reins, we were moving.

And I mean moving fast! Count on our very good God to provide us with horses that seemed like they could have pulled Elijah's chariot!

Charleston quickly faded from view. But I did not slack the pace till we were way, way gone. Then, to preserve the horses, I slowed them down a bit, and we settled into a steady pace. We would go almost all the way tonight. The farther we got from the scene of the "crime," the better chance we would have of keeping Mabel safe until we got back.

Chapter Eleven

I lay there in bed in the wee hours of the dawning light looking at the ceiling of the guesthouse in Walterboro. We had gone to within about an hour of the plantation and stopped the carriage in the deep woods. Obviously, we could not tell Mabel everything, but she clearly trusted us, so we told her enough, "enough" being that we would be gone for several hours, but we would come back, and that she needed to stay right where she was, and by midnight the next night we would have her reunited with her dear Joe.

We had gone several hundred yards away, well out of sight and earshot, and bedded down in the woods. We knew it had to be about four in the morning. We drifted off quickly to sleep, and now I was once more in the safety of a modern-day bed in the modern-day world contemplating not just what would go on during the day in our time but praying over what would go on the very next night so many years earlier.

When everyone was up and ready, we were out the door one more time for another pleasant day in the Lowcountry. We went back to the Olde House Restaurant for breakfast, from there spent some time at the gym, and then it was back to the guesthouse. Mom and the girls spent some time there mending some clothes and doing some school work. I was already ahead on my school work, so I got to go with Dad and Pastor Baker to the local golf course, a great place called Dogwood.

Golf; otherwise known as an excellent way to ruin a good walk.

Whose idea was it, I wonder, to put a tiny white ball on a tiny wooden stick and try to whack it with an oddly shaped club until you drive it into a hole hundreds of yards away, only to pull the ball out of the hole and repeat the entire process seventeen more times? And whose idea was it to put a bunch of water and sand in the way to make that process more difficult?

As you can probably tell, I am not a very good golfer. Of course, Dad really isn't either. Mind you, being about as strong as a gorilla, he can drive the ball three hundred fifty yards or so. But, since the ball never goes straight, he spends a lot of time in the woods trying to find out exactly where it landed.

Pastor Baker won the round easily. Dad finished about fifteen strokes behind him. And, much to my chagrin, I finished one stroke behind Dad. One... Lousy... Stroke. I may not be good at golf, but I don't like losing at anything.

The best part about the entire affair was the hot dog we got at the clubhouse for lunch between holes nine and ten.

We came back to the guesthouse and cleaned up, and all of us spent some time studying or resting. I knew that Dad would be kneeling somewhere over his Bible looking over the message for tonight and praying for God to fill him with the Holy Ghost. So, I spent some time praying that God would answer that prayer for him.

An hour or so before church, we ran into town and grabbed some fast food, and then came back and headed for the church.

Night four of the meeting; what would God do with the service? Dad preached out of Joshua 4. At least that is where he started. He told all about Jericho, that great city the children of Israel defeated when they first crossed over into Canaan. But then he pointed out that God is not just interested in us knowing about cities; God has always been interested in individual people. So, Dad preached on one of those individual people that the Bible specifically named, a harlot called Rahab.

Rahab came to trust the God of Israel. She got saved. Not only did she get saved, Matthew 1 tells us that she ended up in the bloodline of Jesus Christ! Her past was no longer an issue; when she got saved God erased it from the heavenly record.

I just love the way God gives a fresh start; no one can do it like He does it. The world will hold things against you, but God died for all of those things. When a person gets saved, all of the righteousness of Christ is added to their account. When the Father sees them, all He sees is the goodness and purity of His own son, Jesus.

While Dad was preaching, I looked around at what faces I could see. Everyone seemed to be "getting it." And during the invitation, a couple of precious people came down and gave their lives to Christ and received that fresh start that only He can offer.

All of us left church that night walking on clouds, thrilled to be alive, and rejoicing in just how good God is. We got back to the guesthouse, went through our nightly routine, prayed together (those precious moments as a family and the family's God), and then everyone headed to bed. The night had been a complete triumph so far; now we just had to see how the rest of the night would go.

Chapter Twelve

Donkeys. Really? But then again, I guess I am the one who left the fine horse and carriage off up in the woods. Our Conductor just smiled and shrugged and said, "Well, they will definitely get you to where you need to go. Then you can just turn them loose, trust me, they know their way home.

We knelt one more time and prayed to begin our mission on this day, and, of course, the Conductor was gone when we finished. This was day four; we were running up against the clock.

We mounted our long-eared steeds (which we had already affectionately named Huey, Dewey, and Louie) and started off toward where we had left Mabel and the carriage. The only sounds were of our legs brushing up against branches as we passed, and the occasional "Thwap" as one of us swatted an aggressive mosquito.

Everyone was in their own head thinking their own thoughts. But I knew that we were all very likely playing out the same scenarios in our mind. Our task on this day was to get Mabel to the rendezvous point, and then wait for midnight and hope Joe would arrive. If he did, from there we had to get him and Mabel to safety, not temporarily, but permanently.

I suppose it goes without saying that the donkeys were not nearly as fast a means of transportation as the horses and carriage. Nonetheless, Huey, Dewey, and Louie clopped along steadily, and we were grateful for them. And, about three hours into our donkey foray, we arrived at the carriage in the woods.

Mabel was there to greet us.

"You came back," she said simply.

"Of course, we did, Sis, that is what family does."

She smiled the warm smile of a child of God, and I knew she understood. Our skin may be different colors, but all of the saved have the same Father and are joint heirs with Christ. In fact, that was what Carrie conveyed to her last night that instantly let her know she could trust us:

"I have been a born-again child of the living God for nine years; how about you?" Carrie had asked.

"Oh, Child, I came to know Him more than thirty years ago, and He ain't never done me nothing but good!" she had responded.

That was all that it took.

There was still plenty of daylight in the sky, so none of us would be going anywhere anytime soon. We sat down to rest, and we brought some snacks and some water out of our packs to give to sweet Mabel. She was clearly weakened from her captivity, and the food and water brightened her spirits and restored some of her much-needed energy.

We whiled the day away quietly talking, and from time to time Mabel sang one of the old sweet songs, those African-American spirituals that have such a beautiful yet mournful sound to them. Carrie and Aly picked up on the words and the tune and the tone almost instantly, and our area of the Lowcountry woods was quietly filled with Mabel's lovely soprano voice mixed with Carrie's high tenor and Aly's alto.

Somehow, I suspected that heaven would be a lot like this, only louder.

As the sun began to say goodbye to our side of the world once more, the girls and Mabel crawled back into the carriage, and I started off toward the rendezvous point. There was no more singing, no more talking, but I knew beyond any shadow of a doubt that there was a great deal of praying going on.

"Call unto me and, I will answer thee..." I murmured. "Lord, I am calling. By now the word is surely spreading of the escape in Charleston, and the authorities are being alerted. Please give us sight beyond our eyes, hearing beyond our ears, and wisdom beyond our years. Help us to get these two to safety, I pray, in Jesus name, Amen."

An hour later we pulled up to the rendezvous point. The front wheel of the carriage was actually resting on one of those flat rocks. If Joe took that trail, he would end up right here, and as soon as he did, we would take off like all the demons and devils of hell were chasing us. For now, I kindled a very small fire right near the carriage, something that Joe could see if he got within thirty or forty yards of it.

The night grew darker, and the stars begin to twinkle through the treetops overhead. I looked at my watch and realized it was 11:59. And with perfect timing, sixty seconds later a sweet old man walked into the clearing by the fire, and Mabel was the first one who saw him.

"Oh!" she gasped, as she ran into his arms.

"Baby, baby, oh, my sweet baby," he said as he held her and stroked her hair. "I done thought I'd nevermore see you agin. Then these sweet kids done come by, and I been pinnin' my hope on them and the Lord ever since. I just cain't believe you done done it, oh, thank y'uns so much, thank you, thank you."

Mabel just cried and held Joe tight. Carrie and Aly were crying.

I was not crying. Mind you, I wanted to, but I knew we had to move, and the faster, the better.

"I hate to interrupt this, I really do, but we need to go, and we need to go now. We are not out of the woods yet either literally or figuratively. Please, all of you ladies get into the carriage; Joe, if you don't mind, please come up front with me, I could use another set of eyes."

Mabel and the girls instantly complied, as did Joe. I pulled out my compass and set a course due south. It only took thirty seconds or so for Carrie to realize that.

"Hey, Bro? Are you going south? What's up with that?"

Joe's eyes got bigger as if he was suddenly worried again that we were up to no good.

"Yes, Carrie, we are heading south," I explained, "for two reasons. One, all of the pursuit will be heading north. Two, if I remember my history correctly, Beaufort, forty-two miles south of here, is home to a section of the Underground Railroad."

"Yes, Son, yes, it is," Joe said as the smile quickly re-emerged on his face. "We slaves done heard that down by the banks of the Combahee River, folks come through what will help slaves escape to the coast and onto ships headed up north. If'n we can git there, I believe we might jest escape after all, yes sir, I surely do."

"That is my plan, Sir, that is my plan. We will not make it there all the way tonight, but we will get close and stop undercover well out of town back up in the woods. Then my sisters and I will be gone for a good while, but we promise, will be back the next day to help you make contact with the Underground Railroad. Mabel knows she can trust us in this; we left her last night and came back today."

I knew that Carrie and Aly, like me, were probably thinking of our second mission, Free Fall. We had managed to get little Miriam on a ship headed to safety in Sweden. Ohio was not quite so far, but it may as well be a universe away if we could not find a contact to the Underground Railroad. But God had not brought us this far just to let us fail; I was very sure of that.

We drove on through the night and once again stopped at about four in the morning. We bid our friends goodbye and assured them that we would be back the next day. Joe looked over at Mabel, and she just smiled a smile that said, "Yes, you can trust them."

A few hundred yards later we bedded down and quickly went to sleep.

Chapter Thirteen

Day five. It seems like we always tried to wrap things up quicker, but never were able to do so. Oh well, maybe next time. For now, the pressing issue was, of course, my dad. Mr. Up-And-At-Em was wandering through the house singing at the top of his lungs, "I'm siiiiiinging in the rain, just siiiiiinging in the rain! What a gloooorious feeeeeling I'm haaaaaaapy again..."

Ugh. What right does anyone have to be so chipper in the morning?

Mind you, it was not actually raining, inside or out. That was, apparently, just the happy tune on his mind when he woke up.

I rubbed my eyes, stretched my sore legs, and then plopped my feet down on the floor. I could not help but notice that I seemed to be the "bigfoot" of the family; even Dad only wears size elevens, I am wearing thirteens. No matter, though, mom always says, "As long as your feet do their jobs, it really doesn't matter how small or big they are."

I made my way into the bathroom, made myself presentable (at least my version of presentable; mom and the girls often disagreed with me on that one), and joined the family in the kitchen. Then it was out the door, back to the Olde House for another great breakfast, and then on to the gym. Today Dad and I worked shoulders. That meant lots of overhead presses and a ton of shrugs. The girls did whatever they were doing on the machines. Honestly, I would not even begin to try and figure out what those things do; they look a lot like medieval torture devices.

Once we got done, we grabbed a light bite of fast food. We didn't want to eat too much because we knew what was coming next...

We went back to the guesthouse and relaxed for a bit, then at 2:00 Pastor Baker came and picked us all up and took us about fifteen minutes down the road to one of the most amazing places I had ever seen. And yet, with what we were doing at night, it was sort of a scene of mixed emotions for us as well.

The destination was The Longbrow, a lovely former rice plantation. It is now an amazing showplace for horses and agriculture. It is owned by a wealthy businessman who uses it as a vacation home and hunting grounds. I could tell Mom was in heaven as she oohed and ahhed over the lovely old trees covered in Spanish moss that were lining the driveway.

Jo Ann and Joe Ben, those sweet folks from Pastor Baker's church, live on the plantation and manage it.

If you have never gotten to see an old rice plantation, it is well worth your time to do so. Even after the Civil War many of the plantations continued to operate. And oftentimes, especially in the cases where slave owners had actually been kind to the slaves, the slaves chose to stay on and work as employees.

The folks back then were pretty ingenious when it came to engineering. They came up with a system of lochs and levies that allowed them to harness rising water levels and keep the fields constantly wet. Many of those exact same systems, built so very long ago, are actually still in use today, even though rice is rarely grown there anymore. Instead, those areas are home to game birds and alligators.

We actually got to see about a twelve-foot-long mama alligator on her nest!

"Don't y'all get too close, now," Joe Ben said, "Ol' mama there, she'll be might protective of them babies."

We got to go around the fields in his off-road vehicle, and we all gasped in amazement at a flock of one of the prettiest birds I have ever seen, a lovely pink and white thing. Joe Ben said it is called a Rosetta Spoonbill.

We finished up our tour and headed to the house where Jo Ann and Jo Ben live and got to experience a treat, one of my very favorite meals, a Lowcountry boil.

If you have never had a Lowcountry boil, then you have never been right up to the gates of heaven itself. There really is nothing at all quite like it. A low country boil is boiled up in a huge pot. It has potatoes, corn on the cob, sausage, chicken, shrimp, and mussels. It is dumped out on a table covered in newspaper, and you pick it all up and eat it with your hands.

The coolest part of all, in our case, is that Joe Ben caught the shrimp right there in the gullies of the plantation! It is almost like they were trying to get to the house just so that I could eat them; *Hey, fellas, come on and follow me. Let's all go hop in that net so the nice man can catch us and cook us up for some hungry Night Heroes!*

We ate until we were all about to pop. Then, to make things either worse or better depending on one's perspective, Mrs. Jo Ann pulled out a lovely homemade banana pudding.

Did I make room for it? Yes, oh yes...

We eventually said our goodbyes and waddled to the church van. Pastor Baker took us back to the guesthouse, and we started getting ready for church. Man, I was just hoping all of my food would be digested enough for me to go to work tonight after dark!

Dad preached tonight on my favorite person, and his too. He used Matthew 26 as his text and preached on Jesus in the Garden of Gethsemane. Specifically, he dealt with the cup that Jesus mentioned over and over again while He was in agony in that garden. He kept on praying, over and over again, "Father, if it be possible, let this cup pass from me." But then He also said, "nevertheless, not as I will, but as thou wilt."

That cup was God's judgment and wrath that would have to be poured out on someone to pay for all of the sins of all mankind of all time. Someone would have to be punished for what we did. This was a very real debate going on in the garden. Jesus was not being forced to drink the cup; He was being asked to drink the cup. He would either voluntarily choose to suffer for us, or He would say no. If He said no, we were all doomed to spend an eternity in hell.

But He said yes. He said yes! Jesus loved me so much and loved you so much and loved everyone else so much that He said yes to the cup; He said yes to Calvary.

There were not many dry eyes in the house that night, as everyone was able to see so clearly how Jesus in love suffered and died for all of us.

I cannot think of a better way to end a meeting than having everyone turn their eyes on Jesus like that.

When the altars emptied and everyone went back to their seats, the pastor said a few words and concluded the service. Everyone mulled about for a while after that, not quite willing to see everything end. But, as my dad always points out, a revival is not a meeting, it is a change of spirit. That being the case, it can go on and even better after the evangelist has left.

As we walked back to the guesthouse under the artistic Lowcountry sky painted by the hand of my very good God, I whispered a silent prayer of thanks for the meeting, and also a prayer that we would finish up our work just as well as my dad had finished up his.

Chapter Fourteen

"If Dad ever sings that song again, I think I am going to scream," I said as I awakened in the rain-soaked antebellum world that would be the site of the last day of this particular mission.

"Agreed," Carrie said as she shook herself off. We had awakened up in the tree line nestled up against the trunk of an ancient old oak. The Conductor himself was standing by a tree just opposite of us, arms folded, waiting for us to be ready to go. Huey, Dewey, and Louie were there with him, seemingly unaffected by the pouring rain that was dripping off of their long ears and long faces.

"Well," the Conductor said, "you may not be singing in the rain today, but it most certainly is a glorious feeling to be serving the King, is it not?"

"It is, Sir," Carrie said with a smile, "I think we would all find it just a bit more glorious, though, if we had gone to sleep in ponchos last night."

The Conductor smiled back and motioned toward our three mighty steeds. We Night Heroes bowed to pray and poured out our hearts to God one more time asking for success. God came to proclaim liberty to the captives, Isaiah 61:6 says, and hopefully, by the time this day was done we would be able to do so on His behalf for Joe and Mabel.

When we were done praying we rose from the earth and headed for our transportation. The Conductor, of course, was gone. Carrie hopped on Huey, Aly on to Dewey, and I brought up the rear on Louie.

"Not exactly a 'Hi-yo, Silver!' kind of arrangement, is it?" Aly asked with a wry smile.

"No, Pipsqueak, it isn't. But the horses we have waiting for us by the carriage certainly are. I suspect the angels of glory themselves would not mind riding those fine creatures. So, let's just meander out that way and hit the trail running."

It took us about two hours, mostly because of the sloppy conditions, to get to where we had left Joe and Mabel and the carriage and horses. They stepped out of the carriage as we arrived; they had been wise enough to stay inside and stay dry from the rain.

"Good mornin' Young un's, good mornin."

I smiled. "Good morning to you too, Joe, and to you Mrs. Mabel. Are you folks ready to make for Beaufort?"

"Yes, Young Man, we certainly are" the sweet lady said. "We have enjoyed a night of freedom; now we hope to turn a night into a lifetime."

"That is our hope too," I said pleasantly. "But let everyone be absolutely on guard. We have done enough of this to know that things very rarely go as easily or simply as we would like them to."

Joe and I once again crawled into the driver's seat, the girls and Mabel piled into the back again. And with a "Giddyap!" and a pop of the reins, the horses were off.

The trip was not nearly as quick or smooth as we would like. We were picking our way through the trees in a southerly direction and trying to avoid any mud holes or falloffs that could derail our trip. The horses that had been provided to us were exceptional; any ordinary horses would probably not have been able to pull the weight through those muddy trails.

I figured on it taking us about five hours in perfect conditions, eight or so in the sloppy conditions we were dealing with. Rain notwithstanding, the time passed pleasantly. I could hear the girls and Mabel in the back talking and laughing pleasantly together. I smiled as I thought of that. Two white girls from the twenty-first century and a recently freed slave lady from the 19th century fellowshipping together as if they had known each other their entire lives. And why should they not? If the gospel of Christ transcends all racial barriers, it should have no trouble at all transcending time barriers and social barriers either. When we get to heaven, we will sit down and talk with Adam about what it was like in the garden of Eden, we will talk with Noah about what it was like on the ark during the flood, and we will talk with unknown Christians of the Middle Ages about what it was like to follow Jesus through persecution.

Joe and I mostly just rode along silently. I guess guys of all ages are pretty much the same; they are not normally given to long, drawn-out conversation. But it was not entirely silent, we did speak periodically, although I did have to be a bit careful in that.

"So, you ain't yet told me where you young un's come from, and how and why you stepped in to help us. It ain't exactly a normal thing to do, I reckon you know."

I took a moment to gather my thoughts before I spoke.

"We are from North Carolina," I answered honestly. "My dad is a preacher. We are only in the area for a little while, but God made it pretty clear to us that we needed to help. It may not exactly be the normal thing to do, as you mention, but I have found that there are both good people and bad people in every place, in every race, and in every time. We just choose to be some of the good ones, regardless of what is considered 'normal,' because that is what Jesus our King expects of us."

That sort of opened up the conversation between Joe and myself. I enjoyed getting to hear how he came to know Christ as his personal Savior, especially since it confirmed what I said about there being good people in every race and in every time. It had been his first master who won Joe to the Lord when he was a little boy. While being obviously and dreadfully wrong in what he believed the Bible taught about slavery, the man was absolutely correct on the gospel and was intent on seeing everyone he knew come to Christ. He was so out of step with the times that he was the one who had taught Joe how to read, and everyone else on his plantation as well, just so they could read the Bible.

"Yes, oh yes, I did think a lot of Master Tom. He done treated everybody with kindness and was he what introduced me to Jesus. Oh, how we all done grieved the day he died; tuberculosis got him when he was still just 30. If he woulda lived, ain't none of us ever woulda ended up with Master Feeney."

We rode on in silence for a while, and I use the time both to pray and to plan. I did not know exactly what we would be facing when we got to Beaufort. I just knew that somehow we had to secretly make contact with the Underground Railroad and get Joe and Mabel to the people who could get them to safety.

Several hours later we made the outskirts of town, and I pulled the horses and carriage to a stop.

"Okay, folks, I need to know what you have heard about the Underground Railroad around here. Tell me everything you can think of; it could mean the difference between success and abject failure."

It wasn't much, but I hoped it would be enough. Talk among the slaves was that there was a cabin along the banks of the Combahee that would hang two lanterns in the window, one high and one low. If one saw the lanterns in the window like that, it meant that someone from the Underground Railroad was there and was ready to help transport slaves to safety. So, the first thing we had to do was pray that someone was actually there and ready on this night. The second thing we had to do was find it before anyone found us. Boy, saying it that way sounded so simple...

"We can't exactly ride the carriage down river," Carrie said. "And walking all along the banks would take a very long time and expose us to prying eyes."

She was right. And despite the fact that I had been thinking of that, I was stumped as to what to do about it. It was Aly that came to the rescue, in her own unique, indomitable way.

"Why don't we do some wheeling and dealing so we can do some rowing and going?"

I laughed. "Only you, Squirt, only you. Your idea is a good one, except for one thing; the carriage and horses don't exactly belong to us."

"Well," she said, "I would think that carriage and horses in exchange for a boat would be a little bit of an unfair trade anyway. Surely, we could get a decent boat with just the carriage alone. And somehow I suspect that these horses know their way home if we let them go." She went around to the front of the horses, took one that she had named Blackberry by the face, and said, "if we turn you and Whip Cream loose, can you find your way home?"

"Whip Cream? Whip Cream and Blackberry? Seriously?"

Aly looked over at Carrie with a bit of playful haughtiness and said, "Can you think of a better name for a solid black horse and a solid white horse? Let me guess, you would probably call them Salt and Pepper, wouldn't you?"

Carrie just stared at her, and the look on her face told me everything I needed to know. I burst out laughing, and said, "Yep, looks like you nailed her on that one. Salt and Pepper? No, I think Blackberry and Whip Cream are definitely the better two names here. But the question is, no matter what we call them, can they find their way home?"

I kid you not; both of them begin to whinnie and shake their heads up and down at that exact moment.

All five of us burst out laughing at that.

"Okay, it looks like we have a plan. Or at least part of one. The next thing we have to accomplish is to find a place to trade the carriage for a boat without Joe and Mabel being seen."

Chapter Fifteen

Not wanting to take any chances, we scouted around for a while for the perfect hiding place. Having dealt a lot with pursuing Indians, we had learned a thing or two about how to conceal people in the wilderness or wooded areas. After forty-five minutes of looking, we found just the thing. A gnarled old tree right by the river bank had sent its roots over the edge and down toward the water. Moss had grown all over the roots and the tree, resulting in a suspended cubbyhole under the bank by the water that could not be seen unless you looked very closely.

We helped Joe and Mabel into the hiding place and then went back to the horse and carriage. Now it was a matter of getting into town and securing a boat.

As we drove down Main Street, I knew we would not have much trouble finding someone willing to make a trade. The carriage we had been provided was a nice one compared to what else we saw drive by.

Just around the corner from the Methodist Church we hit pay dirt.

"Rhett's Boat Works," Carrie said. "That looks like it will do."

We pulled the carriage up into the courtyard, I hopped down and tied the horses, and we went looking for Rhett. We found him in the two-story building out back, utterly absorbed in sanding on a new boat.

"Pardon me, would you by chance be the proprietor of this establishment?" I asked pleasantly.

The man was thin and gaunt but had a pleasant manner about him.

"Certainly, young man, Rhett Thompson, at your service. What may I do for you and these two fine young ladies to help brighten this wet and dismal day?"

We all returned his smile, and I said, "we are in the market for a small boat, something worthy of a river like the Combahee, here, and we have a fine carriage out front that we are willing to trade for it."

"Hmm, well how about that? Did my wife send you, by chance?"

I was instantly very confused, and more than a little bit concerned. What was the man talking about? Fortunately, I did not have to ask.

"She and I were talking just this morning. She is desirous of a nice carriage to go back and forth to Charleston in. I told her that I didn't think we could afford one just yet, but she and I prayed about it before I left for work, and we just committed that to God's hands, to do as He sees fit. And now here you are claiming to have a fine carriage to trade. May I see it?"

May he see it? Yes, oh yes!

We all walked out to the carriage, and the man was clearly and instantly impressed.

"Look at this carriage, yes... but look at these horses! What magnificent beasts!"

Aly piped up immediately.

"I am sorry, Sir, but Blackberry and Whip Cream are not for sale."

"Blackberry and Whip Cream? You named your horses Blackberry and Whip Cream?"

The man laughed uproariously; that was clearly the funniest thing he had heard in years. When he finally stopped laughing and brushed the tears off of his cheeks, he turned to Aly and said, "I understand, young lady. If I had horses as fine as these, I do not believe that I would sell them either. But it is absolutely not necessary. We have horses, Beverly and I, and the carriage you have is tremendous. I do believe we can work out a fair trade."

And we did. We came to his establishment with a carriage and were soon the proud yet temporary owners of a suitable twelve-foot boat.

"Now, if you don't mind me asking, how exactly do you intend to get your boat to the river since you came here with the carriage and are leaving the carriage and have nothing to pull the boat with?"

Stunned.

How in the world had we three "geniuses" overlooked that?

Rhett laughed again when he saw the looks on our faces.

"I think I can help you with that," he said. "I have a fairly beat up old flat cart over here that you are welcome to take. Even giving you that and the boat, I am still getting a good deal with that carriage. Blackberry and Whip Cream are clearly more than capable of pulling the cart and the boat."

We thanked Mr. Thompson profusely and in a matter of twenty minutes had the horses hooked up to the cart and the boat loaded up on the cart. Then we walked the horses casually out of town as if we had nowhere important to be and were not helping two runaway slaves to run for their lives.

Chapter Sixteen

We arrived at the hiding place just outside of town right about the time that it was getting dark. Between the three of us, we got the boat dragged down to the river, and Joe and Mabel came out of hiding to greet us.

"You young un's done did good, didn't you! That's a nice boat, a nice boat indeed. That should float us right on down the river. If we see the lights, we'll stop, if'n we don't, we'll just keep right on floatin', and see where the good Lord takes us."

I laughed a little at that.

"I love your spirit, Joe, I really do. But what say we pray that won't be necessary. You folks load up; let's go find some lanterns in a window."

I got everyone into the boat, shoved off, took a couple of wet steps and jumped in myself. We quickly caught the middle of the stream and were off and floating. The rain was still falling, though far lighter than before, just sort of a steady drizzle. That, combined with the rippling of the water muffled most other sounds and made for an almost sleepy way to travel.

We began to pass cottages on either side of the banks; tiny huts that most people in our day would think of as storage buildings, but people in this pre-Civil War world doubtless thought of as so very much more. It seemed to me that the river was fading away from town just a bit, and that made me feel a bit of relief. Fewer people meant less curious eyes.

We floated for goodness knows how long, and every cottage seemed the same, cottage after cottage.

"There!"

It was Aly with her keen eyes that saw it first. Left bank of the river, fifty yards ahead, a tiny cottage with two lanterns in the window.

"Oh! Oh, Joe! Is it really real?"

"It is, Baby, it is," Joe said to his dear bride. They hugged and wept as we drew nearer and nearer to the shore and freedom.

With five feet to go, I jumped out, grabbed the front of the boat, and wrestled it to shore. I tied it up, then turned back to the boat and began helping everyone disembark. Mabel, then the girls, then Joe brought up the rear. Once ashore we made for the cottage.

"That will be quite far enough," the wicked voice said from the shadows.

We all froze. I knew that smarmy voice. So did Joe. So did Mabel, and she began to cry as Joe held her.

Mr. Feeney stepped out of the shadows and lit his lantern. That was followed by nine more lanterns being lit, each one garishly illuminating the wet face of whatever very cocky looking man was holding it. At that moment, as if on cue from heaven, the rain stopped, the clouds parted, and the lovely light of the moon shone on everything that was happening.

Ten enemies standing between Joe and Mabel and freedom. Ten potential reasons my sisters and I could never go home again.

"Did you think I was just going to let you go, Property? After the jailbreak in Charleston, a few of the runaways were caught pretty quickly. Others are still loose; they have vanished like the devils they are. Those that were caught, though, with a little good old-fashioned 'persuasion,' were more than willing to tell us what places they knew that slaves would go to in order to make contact with the so-called 'Underground Railroad.' We have dispatched men to every single location. It just so happens to be my good fortune to have chosen this one."

I smiled, but it was an angry smile.

"Good fortune? Is that what you call it? You may not think so when we are done here."

That brought peals of devilish laughter from Feeney and all of his men.

"Boy, what do you take me for, a woman?"

"No," I replied matter-of-factly. "If you were a woman, I would be far more worried."

Carrie and Aly, if they had been drinking milk at that moment, would have spit it out of their noses they laughed so hard. That made Feeney turn red-in-the-face furious, and he started to speak, but I cut him off.

"Oh, shut it, before you say something stupid. Here is how this is going to go. You can turn around and walk away now and save yourself a lot of trouble. Or, you can do as I hope and try to stand in our way, and find yourself beaten down by two former slaves, a boy of sixteen who is already bigger and stronger than you, and two girls, either of which could whip you in a fair fight. You choose."

Hoo boy! Did that set him off! He was literally shaking he was so mad! Just behind me and to my left I saw Aly slip her slingshot out of her pack and load a rock. On the other side, Carrie picked up a boat oar, slammed it to the ground, and broke off the head of it. That left her standing there holding a very solid three-foot stick, with which I knew she was about to do a whole lot of damage. Joe stepped up beside me and flexed arms made hard by years of labor. Mabel stepped to his side, smiled at him, and waited. For her freedom, and for her love, I suspected she was going to be an absolute demon in this coming battle.

Feeney pulled out the same whip I had seen him lash Joe with. I knew he was very good with it. I also knew, as good as Aly is with her slingshot, that he was never going to get the chance to use it.

"Kumitay!" I hissed, and when I did, a war broke loose on the banks of a river.

Chapter Seventeen

For those who do not know, kumitay is a Japanese word. It is one of the first words my dad learned in martial arts. It simply means "fight." When I said that word, the first thing I heard was the "thwap!" of Aly's slingshot. Feeney crumpled like a piece of paper and was writhing on the ground; Aly had plugged him right between the eyes.

Instantly there was pandemonium. Two men rushed at Carrie, and she swept into action. She jabbed the first guy right in the throat then dropped to the ground spinning. She made a complete revolution and caught guy number two right across the knees with that stick, and he cut a complete flip and landed gasping on the ground. She quickly popped up, stick overhead, and brought it slamming down across the top of the head of the next guy, and he was done.

Joe did not wait for anyone to come to him, he charged like a bull and slammed hard into another man, ramming him into the side of the cottage. He began to rip punches into the guy's face, but another guy was instantly right there, and they tumbled to the ground grasping and clawing and punching. Mabel literally dove in and grabbed the second guy by the back of the hair, and I heard him scream in agony as she yanked out handfuls of it.

I was in enough of a mess of my own. If I could reach into the past, I would love for Big Jackson to show up right now, I could have used him![*] I was in the middle of a scrap with three guys. I knew I had to whittle those odds down fast, so I front kicked one in the throat, and he was out for good.

That left me vulnerable, though, and the other two took advantage. They very quickly had me on the ground, and I was covering my face with my arms to absorb the blows.

"Thwap!" went Aly's slingshot again as I heard another man crumple, and that just so happened to be the guy that Carrie had hit in the legs with the stick. He made the mistake of getting up, and Aly made him pay dearly for it. "Thunk!" went Carrie's stick, and I knew number ten had been hit. "Thwap!" again, and one of the guys on top of me rolled off, holding his head and screaming. That gave me the opportunity to reach around my remaining guy's head, grab him by the hair, then put my

---

[*] Another <u>Cry From The Coal Mine</u> reference

other hand under his chin, and twist violently. He rolled off, he had no choice, and I rolled over with him and piled on top of him. One massive punch to the center of his face and his nose was broken, and his night was done.

I whipped to my feet and saw Carrie still battling with one of her first guys who had gotten back up. He had found a stick somewhere and was matching her stroke for stroke.

"Thwap!" and that guy was down too. Carrie did not take time to complain. She turned her attention to where Joe and Mabel were still struggling with their men and went to join them.

The whole battle had only been going on for maybe a minute, and I was whipping from side to side seeing what still needed to be done.

"Pow!" came the fist into my jaw, and I went down to one knee. I had not seen that one coming. Who did I miss?

"It's a good thing I've got a hard head, boy; otherwise, I may miss out on all the fun!"

It was Feeney. And I was glad, oh, so glad. I scanned the yard and saw that our side was rapidly mopping things up. I almost felt sorry for the ones Joe and Mabel were whipping. Joe was having to hold Mabel back!

I got to my feet in time for Feeney to swing again. Instead of stepping away I stepped in, looped my right leg around his right leg, swung my right arm up under his left arm, twisted, and he was airborne, courtesy of a good old-fashioned hip toss. He slammed the ground, rolled onto a knee and started to get up, but I was instantly on his back. I quickly put him in a chokehold, squeezed good and tight and said, "Good night, Cupcake. When you wake up, you will be in your underwear, miles and miles from home, and you will have the Night Heroes to thank for your troubles..."

    Once we tied everyone up, we went inside. Sure enough, as I suspected, there were two ladies and a man tied up and gagged. Feeney and his crew had gotten there far enough ahead of us to imprison them and make everything look normal ahead of our arrival. We untied them and helped them to their feet, as they embraced Joe and Mabel and welcomed them to this stop of the Underground Railroad. A few minutes later we had said our goodbyes, and they all disappeared into the night. I knew they would be safe, now, and soon they would be free, forever free.

    As Carrie and Aly and I made our way into the night, I checked to make sure they were okay. I really shouldn't have worried, I guess, they came through it without a scratch. I was the only one that took a hit, and my jaw was already beginning to feel better.

"Do you really think you should have stripped Feeney to his underwear and sent him downstream tied up in that boat, Bro?"

I was sort of surprised to hear that from Aly, of all people.

"Seriously, Sis? I thought you especially would enjoy the humor in that. Are you maturing, or something?"

She just huffed. "Um, no, and don't insult me. It's just that I'm still carrying the sparklers, Vaseline, and Tabasco sauce."

And then two laughing Night Heroes and one huffing Night Hero went off into the woods to get to sleep and catch our ride home.

Coming Soon:

Terror by Day

There would be no Conductor to guide us, no periods of rest for us to gather our thoughts, and no recovery if we failed. This was all or nothing: and three thousand people would go to a watery grave unless we could figure out a way to stop this. Including us.

Other Books in the Night Heroes Series

Cry from the Coal Mine

Free Fall

Broken Brotherhood

The Blade of Black Crow

Ghost Ship

When Serpents Rise

Moth Man

Other Fiction

Zak Blue: Falcon Wing

Other Books by Dr. Wagner

From Footers to Finish Nails

Beyond the Colored Coat

Daniel: Breathtaking

Esther: Five Feasts and the Fingerprints of God

Nehemiah: A Labor of Love

Marriage Makers/Marriage Breakers

I'm Saved! Now What???

Don't Muzzle the Ox

Romans: Salvation from A-Z

Ruth: Diamonds in the Darkness

Learning Not to Fear the Old Testament

Made in the USA
Coppell, TX
11 April 2022